NEVER TO LET GO

NEVER TO LET GO

Marlene McFadden

Chivers Press • G.K. Hall & Co.
Bath, England   Thorndike, Maine USA

This Large Print edition is published by Chivers Press, England, and by G.K. Hall & Co., USA.

Published in 1999 in the U.K. by arrangement with the author.

Published in 1999 in the U.S. by arrangement with Marlene McFadden.

U.K. Hardcover ISBN 0-7540-3840-8 (Chivers Large Print)
U.K. Softcover ISBN 0-7540-3841-6 (Camden Large Print)
U.S. Softcover ISBN 0-7838-8656-X (Nightingale Series Edition)

Copyright © Marlene E. McFadden, 1998

All rights reserved.

The text of this Large Print edition is unabridged.
Other aspects of the book may vary from the original edition.

Set in 16 pt. New Times Roman.

Printed in Great Britain on acid-free paper.

British Library Cataloguing in Publication Data available

Library of Congress Cataloging-in-Publication Data

McFadden, Marlene E. (Marlene Elizabeth), 1937–
    Never to let go / by Marlene McFadden.
      p. (large print) cm.
      ISBN 0-7838-8656-X (lg. print : sc : alk. paper)
      1. Large type books. I. Title.
    [PR6063.C43N4 1999]
    823'.914—dc21   99–22228

CHAPTER ONE

The big house looked just the same—white painted walls, green shutters folded back, a long sweep of drive leading to the tall, iron gates where Sasha was now standing. She remembered her first sight of the house, Aux Camelias, from the bedroom of the cottage across the road, and turned slightly to look at that, too.

It seemed ages ago that she had stayed here with her parents, but it wasn't so long really, less than twelve months; twelve months during which her whole world had been turned completely upside down. Without being aware of it, she twisted the ring on the third finger of her left hand, feeling the smoothness of the emerald, the small circlet of surrounding diamonds. Emil's ring. Oh, Emil . . .

She took a deep breath. She must go up to the house. She had come so far and there was no turning back. Her mother's words echoed in her ears.

'Are you mad? Please don't do this, Sasha, throwing yourself at him when he obviously doesn't care two hoots for you.'

Sasha had wanted to cover her ears with her hands to stem the torrent of her mother's words.

'Stop it, please,' she begged. 'Emil loves me.

I know he does. There's got to be some reason why he's never shown up. I need to find out what that reason is. Can't you see that?'

Her mother was relentless.

'All I can see is that you're going to make yourself ill again,' she said.

It was true. Sasha had been ill, but that hadn't been Emil's fault. Glandular fever had struck her down, leaving her as weak as a kitten. That was why so many months had gone by before she could get back to Brittany, back to where it had all begun—her meeting with Emil; their falling in love; their promise to marry; the letters; the wedding plans. And then the awful silence, the terrible suspicions building up in Sasha's mind.

In some ways her illness had come as a blessing in disguise, masking and numbing her pain, her humiliation, her fears about what had gone wrong. But now she was well again, and she was here and she couldn't put off the moment any longer.

Walking resolutely up the drive towards the house, she rang the brass bell as she had on that faraway morning. Would Emil answer, looking as he had then, tall, good-looking, with smooth, dark hair and the friendliest brown eyes Sasha had ever seen? And what would he say when he saw her there? What could he say? Or would it be Louise, his strange, ethereal mother who would answer the door?

Not for the first time, Sasha wondered if

Louise had had something to do with Emil's jilting of her, but, as before, Sasha rejected this notion. Louise was strange, certainly, but kind and gentle. She had welcomed Sasha. She had invited Sasha's parents to dinner at Aux Camelias. She had been overjoyed when she knew Sasha and Emil were growing fond of one another, not like Anne, Sasha's mother, who had insisted they were far too young, who had said, wait, think it over, make no commitment.

Sasha pulled herself up sharply, pressing the doorbell again with firmness. Speculation would get her nowhere. She was here. Soon, too soon, she would know the truth. There would be no more questions awaiting answers. Both of them, she and Emil, would have to face the truth. Sasha found herself praying fervently.

It seemed long minutes before the stout, green-painted door was opened and Sasha found herself staring at a complete stranger, a tall, slender woman with short, neat, grey hair. She wore a dress of hyacinth blue, with long sleeves and a flowing skirt that fell well below her knees. The blue of the dress matched exactly the blue of the woman's eyes, as did the string of blue glass beads she wore around her neck.

Sasha put her age at somewhere between sixty and seventy. It was difficult to be more exact because the woman had the enviable figure of a young girl. Only the lines on her face and the veins in her hands gave her age away. Sasha's French was not good. It had been one of Emil's promises to teach her his language.

'After all,' he had said, 'I speak English perfectly, so I think my wife should speak my language, too, don't you?'

'Bonjour, madame,' Sasha began nervously, thrown by the sight of this stranger.

She sought desperately for the right words to continue. The woman smiled, immediately putting Sasha at her ease.

'It's all right,' she said, 'I can speak English. How may I help you, mademoiselle?'

'I'm looking for Louise and Emil LeBlanc. They are mother and son. Last year I . . .'

She broke off as the woman's eyes seemed to lose their friendly light, just as though a cloud had passed across the sun.

'They are no longer here, mademoiselle,' the woman said, her voice taking on a sharp edge, 'and I do not know where they are.'

But Sasha knew instinctively without asking that this woman knew the LeBlancs and it might be presumptuous of her, but she believed the woman did know where Emil and Louise were. She decided to press on.

'Please, madame, I must find Emil. I am engaged to be married to him, but I fear something terrible has happened to him. He wouldn't just desert me. I know he wouldn't.

Please, if you know anything, madame, anything at all, tell me. I'm desperate.'

The woman hesitated, still with her hand holding the door open. Before she could speak, however, another voice spoke from behind her. Sasha recognised only one word, 'Sophie', obviously the woman's name. The first woman turned away from Sasha and spoke in French. Sasha cursed her inability to comprehend.

The second woman appeared at Sophie's side. She was equally as tall, but more heavily built, with almost white hair piled high on top of her head giving her an aristocratic look. She wore dark glasses so Sasha could not see the expression in her eyes, but her lips were thin and set in a firm line, and Sasha's heart plummeted. She was going to fail. They would not help her. She felt tears of frustration and disappointment flooding her eyes.

'How do we know you are who you say you are, mademoiselle?' the second woman demanded harshly.

'I wear Emil's ring,' Sasha replied and thrust out her left hand. 'See, I'm not lying.'

The second woman did not even glance at Sasha's outstretched hand.

'You wear a ring, mademoiselle,' she corrected.

Then the woman, Sophie, surprised Sasha by saying in English, 'Will it do any harm to invite this young woman into the house,

Emilie, and hear what she has to say?'

Emilie's head turned towards Sophie.

'You are too soft for your own good, Sophie,' she said, sounding angry.

'She is upset. Perhaps she has come a long way. Could we not at least offer some refreshment?'

Emilie gave a long sigh.

'As you wish. I know you won't rest till you do your Good Samaritan act.'

She turned and walked straight-backed along the long, narrow hallway, disappearing into a room on her right, the same room where Emil had taken Sasha to meet his mother that day she brought the kitten home.

Sophie smiled nervously at Sasha.

'My sister is wary of strangers,' she explained apologetically.

'I'm very grateful, madame,' Sasha breathed as the woman indicated she should enter the house.

'I am mademoiselle, not madame. We are both unmarried, Emilie and I. You would say we are the Misses Couriol.'

She sounded friendly, and Sasha was glad of this, but did not know how Emilie Couriol would treat her. At least they hadn't slammed the door in her face. Sophie directed her into the room where her sister, Emilie, was now sitting in a high-backed chair facing the long windows which overlooked the front lawns and the high stone wall that hedged the property.

Emilie had her hands clasped in the lap of her long, dark brown dress. She wore no rings, nor jewellery of any kind. She seemed harsh and cold whilst Sophie had a warmth to her.

'I'll make some coffee,' Sophie said and disappeared, leaving Sasha standing awkwardly near the door.

Without looking at her, Emilie Couriol said, 'Please, mademoiselle, sit down.'

Sasha did so, crossing to the sofa, sitting on the very edge. Emilie continued to stare at the windows.

'So you say Emil promised to marry you.'

The words were more statement than question, curtly uttered.

'Yes,' Sasha replied and glanced nervously at Emilie. 'Then you do know him, mademoiselle,' she said softly.

Emilie Couriol's hands tightened their grip on one another. It was the only sign she gave of her annoyance at Sasha's words.

'I did not say that!' she snapped.

'No, I'm sorry,' Sasha stammered.

She had to tread carefully. If the sisters did know Emil and Louise and she was sure they did, then they held all the cards and she needed their cooperation if she was to get anywhere. There was a brief silence. Sasha wanted to ask so many questions, but she daren't. Let Mademoiselle Couriol be the first to speak. She must certainly have questions of her own to ask, whatever her relationship to

Emil.

'You are English,' Emilie stated the obvious, 'so I presume you returned home to await your fiancé joining you. Am I correct?'

'Yes, you are.'

Mademoiselle Couriol had a shrewd mind and Sasha was beginning to like her direct approach.

'And he never came?'

Sasha looked down at her hands.

'No. I heard from him in the beginning. He wrote to me every day, and he sent my ring.'

Her fingers caressed the emerald lovingly.

'But I never saw him again after we said goodbye at Saint Malo.'

The memories were crowding back, the panic, the hurt coursing through her. She couldn't go on. Tears were falling unheeded on to her hands.

Sophie appeared at that moment, carrying a tray with coffee and cream jugs, cups and saucers, a bowl of brown sugar crystals. She set it on a table in front of the sofa. Sasha dashed away the tears quickly with the back of her hand.

'Do you take cream, mademoiselle?' Sophie asked.

'Yes, please. And my name is Sasha. Sasha Hilton.'

Sophie smiled at her, then started to pour coffee into the delicate blue and white cups. Emilie went on as though there had been no interruption.

'I am sorry for you, mademoiselle. It is a very sad story, but can you not just accept that your fiancé simply changed his mind at the last moment?'

Sasha turned on her.

'No, I can't. Emil wouldn't do that to me. We love each other very much.'

'How long exactly did you know one another before you parted?'

'One month,' Sasha said quietly.

'One month?' Emilie repeated.

'I know what you're thinking, but it wasn't like that. We both knew from the moment we first met.'

Emilie's voice took on a kind note.

'How old are you, my dear?'

Sasha's chin jutted stubbornly.

'I'm twenty-two,' she replied.

'You were so young when you met your Emil. And he was himself only twenty-three.'

It took several seconds for Emilie's words to penetrate, during which Sophie crossed to her sister's side with a cup of coffee. Then Sasha's eyes shot wide open.

'If you don't know Emil LeBlanc, mademoiselle, how do you know his age?'

For the first time, the Frenchwoman seemed flustered. She waved a hand crossly at her sister and spoke in French. Sophie hurriedly put the cup and saucer on the round table by Emilie's side and withdrew to go with her own coffee to a chair nearer the window where she sat holding the cup and saucer but not drinking it.

Sasha stared at Emilie waiting for an answer to her question. Emilie did not look at her but reached out towards the coffee cup. Her fingers seemed to be searching and when they touched the delicate china cup she gave a little start. It was then that Sasha realised that Emilie Couriol was blind. Of course! The dark glasses, the habit she had of seeming to stare straight ahead. The knowledge came as a shock.

Sasha felt embarrassed as though her questioning of the Frenchwoman moments earlier had been cruel and insensitive. But she must have an answer to her question, even if she had to ask it again. That proved unnecessary. After lifting the coffee cup to her lips and sipping delicately, Emilie Couriol spoke, her voice once again polite and even.

'Yes, I do know Emil LeBlanc,' she began, 'and his mother, too. They leased this house from us last summer whilst Sophie and I were in Scandinavia.'

Sasha took a sharp intake of breath which Mademoiselle Couriol's keen ears did not miss.

'You believed Aux Camelias belonged to the LeBlancs, mademoiselle?' she queried.

'Well, Emil never said. I just assumed.'

'They were tenants,' Emilie stated shortly.

Be that as it may, Sasha saw a ray of hope.

'So you know where they went when they left here? You have a forwarding address, no doubt.'

Later, Sasha knew that so many things would occur to her—the mystery as to Emil's complete silence was far from solved, but just for now to hear where he and Louise had gone when they left Aux Camelias would be enough for her.

'I am sorry, I have no such address. Indeed, why should I? I hardly knew them.'

'Oh, Emilie!' Sophie spoke for the first time, uttering the words in a distressed, unbelieving voice.

Emilie banged one hand on the arm of her chair. The cup and saucer in her other hand wobbled dangerously. She spoke in rapid French and Sasha looked from one to the other. Emilie was livid and Sophie seemed to cower under her sister's onslaught.

It was easy to see now that Emilie was the elder of the two, the dominant sibling and that her word was law. Once the stream of harsh words had dried up, Emilie had calmed down. She had a mercurial temperament and now spoke quietly but firmly to Sasha again, whilst Sophie sat silent and unmoving, staring downwards.

'We have told you all we know, Mademoiselle Hilton,' Emilie said, 'and we can help you no more. I am sorry.'

Sasha wanted to cry out, 'You're a liar, I don't believe you.' She wanted to appeal to the gentler, more sensitive Sophie. But how could she make such an accusation in their own home? And what good would it do? Emilie wasn't going to weaken, and Sophie would never gather the strength to oppose her sister.

Sasha knew her mission had failed. She was beaten before she had really got started. She stood up abruptly, depositing her untouched coffee cup on the table.

'I don't know why you are treating me this way,' she said, trying to keep her voice steady 'Are you trying to protect Emil in some way? If he did decide he didn't want to marry me and you know this, would it be too much for you to tell me? If he was a coward, do you have to be cruel?'

But she didn't believe what she was saying. She would never believe Emil didn't love her. No matter how illogical it seemed, she would continue to have faith in him. Without that, without trusting him, she had nothing left.

Neither sister spoke as Sasha went on.

'Thank you for allowing me into your home.'

She turned to the door and Sophie immediately got to her feet to follow. Emilie did not say goodbye. As they reached the front door, Sophie touched Sasha's arm gently.

'Forgive us, my dear,' she whispered.

Sasha felt another surge of hope.

'Won't you tell me what's going on?' she begged, speaking as quietly as she could.

Sophie shook her head.

'There is nothing to tell, mademoiselle,' she said.

Sasha tried to catch her eyes but Sophie looked away quickly.

'Goodbye, mademoiselle,' she said, opening the door.

Sasha opened her leather shoulder bag and rummaged for the small white card, one of her father's business cards that bore their address and phone number. She pressed it into Sophie's startled fingers.

'Please, Mademoiselle Couriol,' she urged, 'take this and if ever you feel you can, phone or write, please.'

Sasha couldn't keep the desperation out of her voice. Sophie stared at the business card.

'It will do no good,' she stated blankly. 'Emilie, you see . . .'

She didn't finish her sentence.

Sasha gave her no chance to hand back the card. She fled down the drive and through the tall, imposing gates. She had parked farther up the road and she ran and got into the driving seat, starting up the engine, moving off down the hill towards the village of Melrand. Only when she was well on the road to the town of Pontivy, ten kilometres away, where she had earlier booked into a hotel, did she allow herself to stop the car, and let the hot, bitter tears come freely at last.

She cried for a long time. Then she dried her eyes, staring in the rear view mirror as she dabbed at them. She looked terrible. She had wept so many useless tears. Enough was enough.

She had had such high hopes of seeing Emil again. At worst, she had hoped for an explanation. At best they would have been reunited, the mystery solved, her love for him justified, her belief in his undying love for her sustained.

Now it seemed she had little more than memories. But as she started up the car again she felt a wave of strength, of determination. This couldn't be the end. She wouldn't let it be.

Some day, somehow, she would be with Emil again. She didn't yet know how this would come about, but she must see this episode as merely a temporary setback.

CHAPTER TWO

It was snowing when Sasha drove home from the library, the large flakes falling heavily and giving every indication of settling. It was January and this was the first snow of the winter. At the moment the roads were fairly clear and driving was no problem, but come tomorrow morning, it could be a very different story.

It took about twenty minutes from the town centre to the Hiltons' detached house in a quiet suburb. Sasha went up the drive and parked in the garage next to her mother's car. Her father's space was empty. He didn't often leave his legal offices till six at least, and most evenings had work to do at home on top of the long hours. Sasha hoped he wouldn't have problems with the snow by the time he left.

She let herself into the house. Her mother had been baking, the aroma of apples and cinnamon permeating the air. Could be apple pie for dessert, or maybe her speciality crumble. Whatever she had made, Sasha knew it would be delicious.

She hung her coat in the hallrobe and pulled off her black leather boots. She went into the sitting-room where a cheery fire was crackling in the hearth. The curtains were drawn, shutting out the snow and the darkness. The lamps, pink-shaded, were lit and the whole room invited Sasha to relax in its welcoming warmth. She sank on to the comfortable couch, leaning back and closing her eyes.

'Have you seen your letter?'

Sasha's eyes shot open and she turned to look at her mother who was standing in the doorway, a wooden spoon in her hand.

'Letter? Is there really one for me?'

She had noticed the pile of unopened envelopes on the hall table but hadn't even bothered to glance through them. No-one ever wrote to her, not these days. There was the odd bank statement, or junk mail, but since Emil's letters had ceased, long ago now, actual letters for Sasha were very rare indeed.

Her mother looked serious and Sasha felt a flicker of alarm.

'What is it, Mum?' she asked, sitting up straight.

'The letter's from France,' Anne Hilton stated.

Sasha was on her feet immediately, facing her mother.

'France?'

'You'd better go and open it, hadn't you?'

She turned away and went back towards the kitchen. Sasha followed her with wildly beating heart.

Could it be possible that after all this time, Emil had written to her? Sasha thought of her ring, hidden away in its velvet-lined box. Was it out of sight, out of mind? Not really, as hardly a day went by when she didn't think of Emil and ache for him.

Casting aside the feeling that her mother was obviously not very happy about the letter, and understanding the reasons why, Sasha went to the hall table and went through the post. There it was, the air mail envelope, the typically foreign style writing and way of addressing, but the surge of wild, breathless hope died as quickly as it had been born, because whoever had written this letter it was not Emil. Sasha had never seen this handwriting before.

As she started to tear open the envelope, hope surged again. Perhaps the letter was from Louise. Perhaps Emil had been ill, seriously ill for a long time. After all, Sasha herself had spent weeks confined to the house, too weak to go out, feeble and listless.

With nervous fingers she unfolded the single sheet of thin paper. The writer's address was given as 'Aux Camelias, pas Melrand, Pontivy, Brittany.' Sasha's eyes went to the signature before even glancing at the body of the letter.

Yours very sincerely, Sophie Couriol.

It wasn't Louise then, no letter of explanation, no offer of renewed hope. But why was Sophie Couriol writing to her at all, six months after they had met? Sasha leaned against the hall table as she read.

My dear Miss Hilton,
 I write with a twofold purpose. Firstly to tell you of the death of my sister, Emilie, who had been ill for some time. Even when you visited us in July, we knew of her illness, and that it was only a matter of time. Secondly, I write to invite you to visit me at Aux Camelias. There is something I must discuss with you,

concerning your fiancé, Emil LeBlanc. I never doubted your word, Miss Hilton, and when I see you I will explain my reasons for this. Whilst Emilie was alive, my hands were tied, but now my conscience has urged me to contact you.

I do hope you will find it in your heart to forgive both Emilie and myself for the way we treated you when you were here, and that you will accept my invitation to visit. A brief note giving the date and estimated time of your arrival will be sufficient. The weather here is quite mild for the time of the year. I hope it is so in England. I look forward to hearing from you.

Sasha was stunned but also unable to suppress her excitement. Sophie's letter must mean something! Surely the Frenchwoman wouldn't hold out such sweet hope only to snatch it away a second time. At last she was going to hear what had happened to Emil. She dashed into the kitchen, waving the letter.

'Mum, oh, Mum,' she cried, 'I'm going back to Brittany. I've been invited to stay at Aux Camelias. I'm going to write an acceptance letter tonight. I'll take my winter week's leave. They're very good at letting you take holidays at short notice.'

Anne Hilton held up her hands, and Sasha's voice trickled away.

'Darling, you're beside yourself,' Anne said.

'Who's written to you? Emil? After all this time? I can't believe it. What's he been doing, for goodness' sake? Doesn't he realise what he's put you through?'

Sasha shook her head.

'No, no, not Emil. It's from the Frenchwoman I saw in July, Sophie Couriol. Her sister, Emilie, has died and now Sophie has something to tell me concerning Emil. She says she's now free to speak. I've got to go, Mum. I've got to!'

'And put yourself through more pain, more disappointment? Darling, I'm only thinking of you. I thought you were beginning to forget.'

'Forget? I'll never forget Emil, Mum. Can't you get that through your head?'

'Well, perhaps not just now,' her mother conceded, 'but I thought you were coming to terms with the situation. You've seemed so much better lately.'

'Oh, Mum.'

Sasha hugged her mother.

'I know you love me and are concerned about me, but I can't ignore Mademoiselle Couriol's letter. I have to take this one last chance. And this time, I feel so much more confident. Please be happy for me, Mum. Please.'

Anne held Sasha away from her, regarding her daughter with serious grey eyes.

'I want only your happiness, Sasha, you know that,' she said.

'I know.'

Anne kissed her cheek.

'But be cautious, my darling. Don't build your hopes too high. You may still have to face the simple fact that Emil jilted you.'

'No, I won't ever do that,' Sasha vowed, 'not till there's no hope left. Until every scrap of hope has gone, I'll keep on believing in Emil and loving him. I can't help it, Mum. It has to be that way.'

When she was in bed that night, Sasha took the ring box from the top drawer of her bedside table. She removed the ring and slipped it back on to her finger. She had taken it off on returning from Brittany in July and hadn't worn it since. Now, she vowed she would never again take it off her finger, unless it was to have Emil put a gold wedding band in its place.

She switched off the lamp and leaned back against the pillows, the duvet tucked cosily around her shoulders. She knew sleep would be a long time in coming. Tomorrow, on her way to work, she would post the letter she had already written to Sophie Couriol.

If all went well she would be in Brittany within the week. In the comforting darkness of her bedroom, Sasha allowed her thoughts to run riot. It was hard not to create visions of what could be waiting for her, but she dwelled also on the past, her mind going back to that summer, eighteen months ago, when Emil

LeBlanc had first entered her life . . .

CHAPTER THREE

The cottage they had rented that summer stood in a short terrace of similar properties and farther down on the opposite side of the road were two more small houses and a baker's shop. Apart from that and the large white house with green shutters that Sasha could see from the small dormer window of her bedroom, the road ran long and straight between fields and woods. The trees were mostly pine trees, tall and majestic, rustling now in the warm summer breeze of a beautiful August morning.

It had also been so late when they arrived the previous night that it had been impossible to see much. Now, as she leaned out of the open window, Sasha realised how peaceful it all was, how beautiful the countryside. She was eager to get out one of the bikes that the brochure had promised were available and go for a long ride. If there were really three bikes, then there would be one for each of them. Dad would be no problem, Sasha thought, but believed her mother might take some persuading.

Her eyes wandered back to the large white house. It was set well back from the road in extensive gardens, neat and well maintained, with a high boundary wall and two huge black painted gates which were stood open. As Sasha stared, she saw a small, fluffy black kitten suddenly appear as if from nowhere between the gates. For a couple of moments, it stood there, as though wondering whether to venture farther, then sprang forward straight into the middle of the road, where it promptly settled down and started pawing playfully at a leaf.

Sasha had no idea, of course, if this particular road was busy with traffic or not. Certainly no noise of traffic had disturbed her slumbers, but animal lover that she was, she wasn't going to take any chances. She ran from the room and down the steep, wooden stairs. As she reached the front door her father was just coming through it, armed with two long French loaves, a carton of milk and a folded newspaper.

'Hey, what's the rush?' he asked, smiling at Sasha.

'Did you see the kitten, Dad?' Sasha asked.

'What kitten?'

'A little black one. It came from the big house opposite. It's just sitting in the middle of the road.'

John Hilton shook his head.

'I never saw it. Aren't you coming for any breakfast?'

'In a minute.'

Sasha pulled open the heavy front door and her father went through the inner door that led to the living-room and kitchen. The kitten was still there and as Sasha approached, slowly so as not to scare the tiny creature, it looked at her and, far from running away, it bounded towards her. She picked it up, disregarding completely all cautionary tales of not handling strange animals abroad. It was very thin. She could feel its tiny ribs under the fluffy fur.

'Oh, you darling!' Sasha cried, and a pair of bright blue eyes stared trustingly up at her. 'Are you hungry? I bet you'd love a saucer of milk, wouldn't you?'

The kitten mewed, just as if it understood what was being said. Sasha half turned back towards the cottage, then hesitated. Her mother would have a fit if she presented them with a new member of the family, and really it would be a foolish thing to do, because Sasha knew how quickly she would become attached to the kitten and then what would happen when it was time to go home?'

She walked back across the road towards the gates leading to the big house. That was where the kitten had come from so presumably it must live there. She could, she supposed, put it back inside the gates, but wouldn't it simply come back out and endanger its life once again? The best thing was to go up to the house and hand the kitten over to its owner.

Holding the little warm body firmly in her

arms, Sasha walked up to the house. It had a fresh, clean look about it. Paintwork gleamed; the brass door bell shone from vigorous polishing; windows sparkled. She did not hesitate before placing her finger on the doorbell and pressing firmly.

It was opened quickly, as though whoever lived there had been just behind the door. Sasha was very taken aback when she was confronted by a young man, casually dressed in a checked, open-necked shirt and blue jeans. He was tall, slenderly built with dark brown hair that fell boyishly across his forehead. He seemed to appraise Sasha, his deep brown eyes moving over her. Then he smiled which made his eyes positively dance and Sasha stupidly felt a hot flush staining her cheeks.

'Bonjour, mademoiselle,' he said and looked at the kitten in her arms.

Sasha decided to speak in English and cross her fingers he would understand her. Her French was of the schoolbook variety! She felt embarrassed enough as it was without making things worse. She held out the kitten.

'I've brought your kitten back, monsieur,' Sasha said. 'He was sitting in the middle of the road and I thought he might be in danger of being run over.'

The young man reached out and took the kitten from her, stroking it gently behind its ears.

'That is very kind of you, mademoiselle,' he

said, 'but this is not my kitten.'

She might have known it! She had had a feeling, because of its thinness, that the kitten was a stray. Now what did she do?

'The poor thing is half starved,' the young man went on, 'so probably it is lost. But you could, I suppose, try the bakery. Maybe they know who owns it. Are you staying in one of the cottages?'

Sasha stared up at him.

'How did you know?'

'Guesswork. You are English. Melrand village is a mile away. No-one lives permanently in any of the houses across the road.'

'We only arrived last night,' Sasha admitted.

She was beginning to wish she had left the kitten where it was and not interfered. Now the onus was going to be on her to find out where it belonged.

'You look worried, mademoiselle. Listen, I will take the kitten and try to find out whom it belongs to, if you like.'

Sasha looked at him.

'And if you don't find out?'

The Gallic shrug came again.

'Then I will adopt it!' he stated simply.

Sasha felt relief flooding through her. She should now say her thanks and go back across the road, but for some ridiculous reason, her feet had become blocks of stone and she felt powerless to move. A fluttery sort of panic was starting in the pit of her stomach and an inner voice was saying, 'If you let this man go back into his house and shut the door, you might never see him again.' Suddenly the thought of that was unbearable.

What was the matter with her? She had never felt like this before, certainly not over a person she had only just met, a foreigner, at that, of whose language she knew only a smattering.

'You are all right, mademoiselle?'

A note of concern had entered the young man's voice.

Sasha pulled herself together.

'Er . . . yes . . . er . . . thank you.'

As she forced her leaden feet to take the first steps away from the house she heard a woman's voice speaking from the hall behind the man.

'Emil, Emil,' and then came a torrent of French.

Emil? Was that his name? It suited him, Sasha thought dreamily. The woman sounded most anxious and Emil turned to look backwards, still holding the kitten tightly in his arms.

'Maman,' he began in a soothing voice.

Once again Sasha could not understand what was being said, but she did understand the woman must be Emil's mother and when she heard the words, 'Fermez la porte, fermez la porte,' she knew Emil was being urged to shut the door.

The brightness of the morning sun was making the interior of the hallway dim and shadowy, and Sasha saw only the outline of the woman who appeared to be as slenderly built as her son and almost as tall. Her hand came to rest on Emil's shoulder. She spoke again and Sasha detected once more the urgency, almost the fear in her voice. But then she saw the kitten and suddenly she was different. She stepped into full view, her face breaking into a smile.

She had a lovely face and large amber-coloured eyes. Her hair was the same tawny shade, held back in a pleat by an ornate wooden slide. She was certainly a very beautiful woman. After stroking the kitten, she turned to Sasha, eyeing her shrewdly as though sizing up whether she could be trusted and pondering what her motives for coming to the house had been.

'You are English, mademoiselle?' she enquired politely.

'Yes, I am. My name is Sasha Hilton.'

The woman gave a brief nod of acknowledgement but did not attempt to introduce herself. Instead she spoke again in French to her son. He then looked at Sasha.

'Please, if you will excuse us, mademoiselle,' he said. 'And do not worry about the kitten. I will take good care of him.'

Politely he withdrew inside the house, his

mother at his side, and closed the door. Sasha stood there for several moments before moving off with a curious sense of unease. So that was that, end of story. The house, which the carved wooden plaque by the side of the door revealed was called Aux Camelias, may be just across the road from their holiday cottage, but Sasha was willing to bet a pound to a penny that that was the last she would see of Emil, whoever he was.

She couldn't have been more wrong. She spent a quiet but enjoyable morning exploring the nearby town of Pontivy with her parents, where her mother did some grocery shopping. Once back at the cottage, Sasha helped her mother to unpack the various carrier bags. She glanced out of the window at her father who was admiring the small, enclosed rear garden, beyond which were open fields with just a couple of properties, perhaps farms, in the distance.

'Do you think Dad will go for a bike ride with me this afternoon?' Sasha asked.

Her mother smiled.

'Have you seen the state of those bikes?' she asked. 'You wouldn't get me on one, I can tell you. Probably the brakes won't work.'

Sasha laughed.

'We could go all along the river bank. That should be safe enough.'

'Well, I fancied going into Josselyn,' Anne admitted. 'And I think your dad does, too.

There's a wonderful castle there, I understand.'

John came back into the kitchen.

'Nice garden,' he remarked. 'It's a real suntrap. I might just settle out there on that bench later with my paper.'

'I think Mum has other plans for you,' Sasha said ruefully.

'Oh, yes? And what might they be?'

'A drive to Josselyn. I want to see as many places as we can whilst we're here.'

'We've got a whole month, love,' John reminded his wife gently.

But Sasha knew once her mother had set her mind on something there would be no budging her. She also knew that her father didn't really mind. He was an easy-going man. At home, he worked long and hard. On holiday, he relaxed and because he knew these were days for being a family together, he would drift along quite happily in whichever direction he was lead. But Sasha was determined to take that cycle ride.

'If you don't mind,' she said, 'I think I'll risk one of the bikes. The exercise will do me good.'

John put his arm around his daughter's shoulders.

'You're too skinny as it is. You don't need exercise,' he said.

Sasha nudged him affectionately.

'Everybody needs exercise,' she told him.

'By the way,' John went on, 'what happened about the kitten?'

Now why should the mention of the kitten cause Sasha's cheeks to grow hot? Well, she knew the answer to that question, but she hoped her parents wouldn't see her blushes. She had not told them of her visit to Aux Camelias.

'Oh, I put him back in the garden where I first saw him.'

Sasha told the white lie with a little niggle of guilt.

'What kitten was this, then?' Anne asked curiously.

'Some creature Sasha rescued from death on the highway,' John teased.

'So long as she didn't bring it back here,' Anne said warningly.

Sasha laughed off the incident. As soon as she could, she got one of the bikes from the shed adjoining the cottage. John looked it over keenly, testing the brakes and the bell. It seemed perfectly all right. The tyres were sound with no pumping up necessary. With her parents watching from the doorway, Sasha rode confidently off down the road towards the river.

*   *   *

The path along its edge was wide enough to take a car so there was no need to be nervous.

Beyond the path was yet more pine forest. The river moved slowly. Sasha rode steadily, enjoying herself. The sudden sound of a loudly ringing cycle bell made her jump and she quickly moved towards the edge of the path.

A young man sped past on a blue bicycle, but he didn't go far and when he stopped and turned to smile at her, Sasha realised that it was Emil. He watched her with interest as she rode towards him, but he would not be aware of the rapid fluttering of her heart. Was this meeting accidental? Emil soon put her straight.

'I hope you do not mind, but I followed you. I saw you from the house.'

He must have left immediately he saw her. She didn't mind, in fact she was very pleased. If he had followed her then surely he must like her and the feeling was mutual.

'How's the kitten?' she asked, not knowing how else to continue their conversation.

Emil smiled.

'Oh, she is fine. My mother has taken to her and calls her BonBon.'

'So he was a she then?'

'Oh, yes. Maman found that out almost immediately.'

'Are you keeping her?'

'It would seem so. I asked everyone possible and no-one knows whom she belonged to.'

Sasha was glad. Knowing that Emil was an animal lover made her like him even more. He got back on his bike.

'Well, shall we continue our ride?' he suggested.

It was uncanny how much at ease they were with one another. They rode along side by side and Sasha was very much aware of his good looks, his slim brown hands holding the handlebars. How old was he? He couldn't be more than about twenty or twenty one. Was he on holiday as she was or did he have a job of some sort?

'Is this your first visit to France, Sasha?' he asked presently.

So he had remembered her name! She felt a warm glow.

'Yes,' she answered. 'We've taken the cottage for a month. My parents and I, that is.'

Emil looked pleased as he replied, 'A month! I will be able to see you often then, won't I?'

Sasha smiled shyly.

'Do you want to see me?' she asked.

'Oh, yes, I do. But if I am a nuisance ...' His voice trailed off.

'Oh, no, not at all,' Sasha assured him, 'but won't you have to go to work?'

She wanted to find out as much as she could about him without making it too obvious. He turned his head away and stared straight ahead and it seemed to Sasha that he withdrew ever so slightly from her.

'I do not work now,' he said quietly.

Which meant, probably, that he had had a job at one time. Had he been made redundant? Job losses must be as prevalent in France as they were in Britain.

'I'm sorry,' she murmured.

He must have guessed what she was thinking because he laughed and the serious moment was gone.

'Oh, I have not lost a job,' he said. 'I gave it up, to look after Maman.'

'Your mother is ill?'

'No, not ill,' Emil said lightly as though it was a matter of no consequence.

He started to pedal faster, bending forward over the handlebars.

'Let's race!' he cried and Sasha knew he had told her as much about himself as he intended doing, for the time being.

They got back to the cottage about an hour later. By that time Sasha was feeling the strain of their long cycle ride but Emil was not even out of breath.

'Tomorrow we will cycle all the way to Pontivy,' Emil declared.

'Oh, will we?' Sasha retorted, secretly pleased he wanted to see her again so soon.

'We can take the riverside path all the way. You will enjoy it.'

'I'm sure I shall.' Sasha smiled. 'Thank you so much, Emil, for your company.'

He gave her a little bow.

'My pleasure,' he said.

She tried the door handle and discovered the door was locked. Of course, her parents wouldn't be back from their afternoon out yet. She groaned.

'You have no key?' Emil asked.

'No, there's only one available. I never gave it a thought.'

'Now you must come home with me. We will have coffee with Maman.'

Remembering how eager Emil's mother was to get rid of her last time, Sasha did not think that was a very good idea, but Emil insisted and they wheeled their bikes across the road to Aux Camelias. Leaving them propped against the side of the house, Emil led the way inside.

The hallway was high-ceilinged and cool and there was a sweeping staircase straight ahead covered in rich, red carpeting. Light flooded on to the long landing through high windows.

'Maman,' Emil called out and put his head around a cream painted door on the right.

Emil spoke in English, for her benefit, Sasha supposed.

'I have brought Sasha to meet you, Maman. She wishes to see how BonBon is settling in. Isn't that kind of her?'

Emil's mother was sitting in a chair by the window. She half rose, but Emil pushed her back again gently, kissing her fondly on the cheek. He beckoned Sasha forward.

'Sasha, this is my mother, Louise LeBlanc.'

Sasha put out her hand.

'How do you do, madame?' she said.

Madame LeBlanc's glance was polite. She even managed a small smile but soon her amber eyes were shifting nervously towards her son. He patted her hand.

'It's all right, Maman,' he soothed her. 'Sasha is our friend.'

'Won't you sit down, mademoiselle?' Louise spoke at last.

Sasha sat on the deeply-cushioned sofa.

'Merci, madame,' she said, 'but, please, won't you call me Sasha?'

'A very pretty name.'

'Thank you.'

'I will make coffee,' Emil declared.

Immediately his mother got to her feet.

'No, Emil, I will do that!' she cried.

She doesn't want to be alone with me, Sasha thought, as once again, Emil urged his mother back into her chair.

'No, Maman, I will do it. Please, everything is all right.'

It was as though he had to be constantly reassuring her. He left them there and Sasha was wondering what to talk about when BonBon suddenly appeared from behind Louise's chair, leaping into her lap, pawing playfully at her hand.

As had happened earlier when Madame LeBlanc had first seen the kitten in Emil's arms, her manner changed. She laughed and rolled BonBon on to her back, tickling her tummy. She cooed over her, speaking softly in French.

'You obviously like cats, madame,' Sasha ventured.

'Oh, yes.'

The amber eyes were warm and friendly now.

'I have always liked them. When I was a child, we had three, and Emil and I had one when we lived in Paris, but sadly it died.'

'You lived in Paris?' Sasha asked politely.

The light darkened in Louise's tawny eyes.

'I don't want to talk about Paris,' she said shortly.

Sasha said nothing, wishing Emil would come back. The wild swings of his mother's moods were disturbing. Was she perhaps mentally ill? Is that why Emil had had to give up his job to take care of her?

The kitten was once again taking Louise's attention. She lifted her up and held her close against her face.

'Ma petite BonBon,' she said lovingly.

She had a strange, childlike quality about her and now that Sasha was able to study her closer, she saw that Madame LeBlanc also had a very delicate appearance, as though a strong puff of wind might blow her away.

Sasha was glad when Emil appeared with a tray of coffee things, whereupon Louise sprang into life and insisted on playing hostess. As she poured coffee and added cream she started to talk to Sasha.

'Emil tells me you are on holiday, Sasha,' she began. 'It is very beautiful around here, n'est ce pas?'

'Very beautiful,' Sasha agreed, accepting the coffee.

BonBon had settled quite happily before the huge, open fireplace, stretching out and closing her eyes. Emil came and sat by Sasha.

'We have been for a bicycle ride, Maman,' he said.

Louise resumed her seat. Her smile was gentle.

'That is good. Where did you go?'

'Along the riverbank. Not very far.'

Louise seemed to be accepting Sasha's presence in the house as though it was the most natural thing in the world. Sasha, for her part, was very much aware that Emil was sitting very close to her, so close that she could easily put out her hand and close her fingers over his. Her own temerity made her blush, and she took a long drink of the rich, creamy coffee.

When Louise suddenly said, 'Why don't you and your parents come to dinner one night?' Sasha was startled.

'Why, that's very kind of you,' she stammered.

'Not at all,' Louise said lightly. 'It is high time we entertained again, don't you think so,

Emil?'

He did not smile and Sasha believed he was not too keen on the idea. She felt a little niggle of disappointment, but his mother went on talking, fast and excitedly.

'Yes, I think it's a wonderful idea. We have hardly seen anyone since we came here. When would you like to come? Tomorrow?'

'Well . . .' Sasha hesitated.

She didn't know what her parents would have to say if she presented them with a fait accompli.

'Good.'

Louise clasped her hands together like an excited child.

'That is settled. Tomorrow it shall be. Emil will drive into Pontivy in the morning to buy all I shall need, won't you, mon petit?'

Still without smiling Emil said, 'Of course, Maman, if it's what you want.'

'Why shouldn't it be what I want? You are being silly.'

'Then I am very happy.'

At last Emil's face lost its tense expression. He turned to Sasha.

'It will be a great honour to meet your parents, Sasha,' he said and the look in his dark brown eyes seemed to say so much.

Sasha was pleased she was going to see Emil again but apprehensive about telling her mother and father that she had accepted an invitation on their behalf. She would now have to explain how it was she met Emil and his mother in the first place, and could only hope that John and Anne had forgotten her white lie about the kitten.

Later, as Emil walked her to the door, leaving Louise once more playing with the kitten, Sasha said, 'Doesn't your mother drive?'

'Yes, she does,' Emil answered, looking puzzled. 'Why do you ask?'

'Because you are the one going to do the shopping. My mother wouldn't dare let Dad loose with a shopping list, not by himself.'

Once again the shadowed look crossed Emil's face.

'My mother does not leave the house,' he said.

'What, never?'

'No. Please, Sasha it is of no consequence.'

Without warning he leaned towards her and kissed her on both cheeks.

'There! And I will not apologise for doing that.'

She didn't want him to apologise. She was delighted and she walked on air across to the cottage. She liked him! And she believed he liked her. She found she could hardly wait to see him again.

CHAPTER FOUR

Sasha knocked gently on her parents' bedroom door and put her head round.

'Ready?' she asked cheerfully.

John was knotting his yellow woollen tie which he wore with a cream coloured shirt. He had a pleasant air of spicy aftershave around him. Anne was fiddling with her pearl stud earrings in front of the dressing table mirror.

'I don't know if I'll ever be ready for this,' Anne murmured.

'You're only having dinner with a very charming Frenchwoman and her son,' Sasha said, 'not visiting the dentist.'

She came farther into the room. John's eyes appraised her.

'New dress?'

'Yes, do you like it?'

Sasha circled showing off her silky pale blue dress. It was the first time she had worn it. She had nearly left it at home, thinking there might be no occasion to dress up but was now very glad she had brought it. Up to now Emil had only seen her in cotton trousers and T-shirts. Tonight she would wear the dress in his honour. She had also loosened her dark auburn hair from its usual pony tail and it shone in soft waves on to her shoulders.

'I suppose it is nice of Madame LeBlanc to

invite us,' Anne conceded, 'but I would have preferred a little more notice perhaps.'

She moved away from the dressing table, the tiny pearls now in place in her ears. Anne, too, had put on a summery dress. At last they were ready and left the cottage.

It was a warm, pleasant evening, the streaks of pink in the western sky promising yet another good day to come. Sasha was beginning to feel nervous despite her joyous anticipation of seeing Emil again.

She had told her parents what nice people Madame LeBlanc and her son were, and had deliberately played down Louise's strangeness and neither had she given any indication that she had really flipped over Emil. She knew she would receive merciless teasing from her father over what he would term a holiday romance and that her mother would take everything far too seriously.

It was Emil who opened the door for them. He, too, was wearing a shirt and tie and smart dark blue trousers. Sasha could see he had made a valiant attempt to restrain his unruly hair. He gave John and Anne a friendly smile, shaking them warmly by the hand, as Sasha introduced them, urging them to come inside. When he turned to Sasha he seemed at a complete loss for words until he caught her hand, bending over it and kissing it gently.

'Sasha, you are so beautiful,' he said.

As they stepped into the hall, John

whispered in Sasha's ear, 'Aye, aye, he's smitten!'

She could cheerfully have kicked his shin.

Madame LeBlanc was in the kitchen which was giving off all sorts of interesting, appetising aromas. Emil took them into the drawing-room, and Sasha could see her mother was very impressed by what she had seen so far.

'A glass of wine perhaps, madame, monsieur?' Emil offered.

'Thank you, that would be very nice.'

Sasha's mother was being formally polite. Sasha hoped she and her father would eventually relax but it all depended on Louise's entrance. If she came in bursting with confidence and warmth, things could get off to a good start. However, if she had that nervous uneasiness about her, Sasha knew it would make her mother, at least, most uncomfortable.

Her fears were groundless. Madame LeBlanc was at her most ebullient all evening and Sasha really began to wonder if she had imagined Louise's nervousness. There certainly was no trace of it that evening. Of course, BonBon's innocent mischievousness was a great icebreaker and it wasn't long before Sasha felt her mother's stilted politeness begin to wane.

'The meal is now ready,' Madame LeBlanc said eventually, and they all went into the dining-room, Sasha's first sight of that room.

'Oh, how lovely!' Anne breathed.

'Why, thank you,' Louise said graciously. 'Aux Camelias is a very lovely house. We are so lucky to be living here.'

They sat down at the long, dark-wood table. Sasha was pleased to discover Emil was placed opposite her, so she could look at him as much as she wanted to!

'Have you lived here long, madame?' Anne enquired as their hostess brought in a large tureen of steaming soup and began to ladle it into shallow white dishes.

'Not long. Only since the beginning of summer, and please you must call me Louise. We must not be formal with one another.'

'And you must call us Anne and John.'

'Oh, yes.' Louise smiled. 'I fully intend to do that.'

They all laughed. Sasha caught Emil's admiring glance as she took the first delicious taste of soup.

'Wonderful!' she praised.

'I am a great cook, is that not so, Emil?'

'The best!' Emil agreed smiling indulgently at his mother.

There was a great rapport between them, especially tonight, and conversation flowed easily throughout the meal. John was a naturally quiet person, in fact Sasha had often wondered how he managed to represent his clients in court, but tonight he responded to

Louise's lead. And Anne was practically eating out of Louise's hand. Sasha was more than pleased with the way events were moving.

They were starting on the fine Brie cheese served with savoury biscuits and piquant slices of apple when Louise said, 'Oh, this is marvellous! Why have we not had guests to dinner before, Emil?'

'I really cannot say, Maman,' Emil replied.

He was ever polite, ever deferential and Sasha knew her mother was quite won over by him. She herself was very quickly becoming deeply fond of him.

'We must make this the first of many such occasions,' Louise went on. 'In Paris entertaining was part of our way of life.'

'You came here from Paris?' John asked, reaching for the cheese board a second time.

As Paris was thrown so casually into the conversation Sasha waited with baited breath for Louise's reaction, remembering how she had shut up like a clam yesterday when Sasha had asked a similar question to her father. Now Louise merely smiled at John.

'Do I detect a note of surprise in your voice, John?'

'Well,' John began, 'I don't wish to decry this part of Brittany, it's very beautiful, but so far removed from what I should imagine Paris to be like, though I must confess I have never been there.'

'I was born in Paris,' Louise told them,

wiping her fingers delicately on the damask napkin that matched the placemats, 'and so was Emil.'

'But we have adjusted to country life,' Emil remarked. 'As you say, John, it is quiet around here.'

'And you wouldn't go back to Paris?' Anne asked.

The Hiltons themselves lived in a quiet suburb of a busy Yorkshire town, but they had every amenity they could wish for practically on their doorstep. Louise looked at her son as though expecting him to have the answer to Anne's question.

'Not in the foreseeable future,' Emil said, at the same time picking up the glass fruit bowl and holding it out to Sasha. 'Another apple, Sasha,' he asked, 'or maybe a few grapes?'

She declined his offer.

'I couldn't eat another morsel,' she said.

Emil got to his feet.

'Then may I suggest that we go to the drawing-room for coffee?'

The subject of Paris was closed. Sasha now knew a little bit more about Emil and his mother but there were other questions still unanswered, not the least being how they could afford to live in this beautiful house when neither of them seemed to have any means of earning a living.

It might have been the excellent wine she had taken with dinner, but Sasha spent the second half of the evening in a sort of haze.

Consequently, she found herself spending long moments staring dreamily at Emil, taking in his every movement, the way he smiled, the way he moved his hands, the endearing gesture he had of brushing back his hair. She sank back against the cushions of the comfortable sofa, surrounded by a euphoric haze of happiness and contentment. Why couldn't this go on for ever? Why did there have to come a time when she and Emil must part?

Occasionally, she caught his glance and their eyes seemed to lock together. She longed to have an opportunity to be alone with him. She could almost feel his arms around her, his soft lips on hers as he drew her close against him.

She sat up straight abruptly, running her hand across her forehead. She picked up her half-filled coffee cup and gulped down the dark, stimulating contents. She must not get carried away. It must be the wine, but in the next instant she knew it was much, much more than that.

As it turned out, her parting from Emil was as formal as it could possibly be. He shook hands with all three of them as they took their leave around eleven thirty.

'Well, thank you very much for a wonderful evening,' John said for the three of them.

'It's been our pleasure,' Louise said, staying in the hallway, not venturing out on to the terrace before the front door as Emil had done.

'Next time it's our turn,' Anne said. 'You must let me repay the compliment.'

Remembering that Emil had told her his mother never left the house, Sasha waited for Louise to show some reaction to Anne's invitation, but she merely said, 'Thank you. Emil and I would like that.'

As they started down the drive, Emil called out, 'Sasha!'

She turned. He stood in the doorway, his hands in his pockets. Her heart seemed to expand till it filled her entire chest.

'Yes?' she breathed expectantly.

'Come round in the morning for coffee, if you like.'

'Yes, I will.'

Sasha walked home, counting the hours till the morning. As they let themselves into the cottage, Anne declared, 'Well, my word, wasn't that something?'

'Fine-looking woman,' John said.

'Beautiful,' Anne agreed, 'and Emil's a good-looking young man. I wonder where Monsieur LeBlanc is.'

'Perhaps he's dead.'

'Or perhaps they're divorced. They must be very well off.'

Sasha listened fondly to them gossiping, knowing how impressed they had been. When Anne turned to her and said, 'You like Emil, don't you?' Sasha felt herself reddening. Before she could reply, John chuckled.

'They couldn't keep their eyes off one another!'

Anne frowned.

'Sasha, you don't intend spending all your holiday time with Emil, do you?'

Sasha tried to appear unconcerned.

'I don't know. I might.'

'But surely he has a job of work to do.'

'No, he hasn't. He looks after his mother.'

Anne slipped off her high-heeled shoes.

'What do you mean, he looks after her?' she asked.

'Well, I don't know really, but he doesn't work. Perhaps he doesn't need to.'

'Lucky him!' her father said with a grin. 'Well, I'm for bed.'

Anne suppressed a yawn as she spoke.

'Just remember, Sasha darling, you're on holiday and you have to go back to England. Don't get too wrapped up with Emil. He seems very nice, but I don't really want you spending all your time with him. We're going to Vannes tomorrow. There's a big aquarium there. Should be worth looking at. Come with us, will you?'

Sasha smiled.

'I might.'

But she knew if there was any sort of a chance of being with Emil, she would not go with her parents.

CHAPTER FIVE

'I'm only going for coffee, Mum,' Sasha explained, unable to meet her mother's direct gaze.

'Then you're coming straight back?'

Sasha looked down, unable to answer the question.

'Later, yes, I suppose so,' she said finally.

Anne turned away, clearly annoyed.

'I can see how this holiday is going to turn out. Your dad and I'll be doing things together and you'll be with Emil all day and every day.'

John came in from the kitchen where he had been helping to dry the breakfast dishes.

'Hey, don't you like being alone with me?' he challenged, pretending to be hurt.

'You know it isn't that, John.'

'You like the boy, don't you?' John went on.

'I don't dislike him. I've no reason not to like him. He's very polite.'

'Then let the two young people enjoy themselves.'

'Thanks, Dad,' Sasha breathed in relief.

'Mind you,' her father said, 'we want to know where you're going and what you're doing. No wandering off and not showing up till the small hours.'

'No, of course not,' Sasha promised, wishing her parents didn't treat her as if she was a young child.

She escaped as soon as she could, making the beds and tidying up her own room before she did so. Whatever Emil had in mind for them today would be good enough for her, but she would make sure she kept her promise to her parents. She didn't want to get into their bad books. She was sure Emil would understand she had to be fair to them.

As she walked up the drive of Aux Camelias, her step was light. Madame LeBlanc's behaviour the previous night had led Sasha to believe she must have been seriously wrong about the Frenchwoman, and she was sure that this morning she would be welcomed warmly into the house. But then she noticed that the green shutters were closed at all the front windows.

She hesitated. Even if they had been closed the night before, which seemed unlikely in this warm summer weather, surely Emil and Louise would be up and about by this time, and not want to keep the daylight out of the rooms. It must be very dark inside with the heavy wooden shutters closed.

With an inexplicable aura of impending doom, Sasha rang the doorbell. It seemed a long time before the door was opened by Emil, an Emil with a strained white face, and sombre, dark eyes. He seemed surprised to see her there and, stepping outside, he closed the door firmly behind him, standing with his back against it.

'Sasha,' he said.

'Is there something wrong, Emil?' Sasha asked. 'You did ask me to come round this morning, for coffee.'

'Yes, I did, but I can't ask you in. I'm sorry. It's Maman. She is . . .'

He seemed to run out of words.

'Is she ill?'

Sasha's voice was anxious whilst the happy feeling that had been present when she awoke that morning was rapidly fading away.

'No, not sick anyhow, but I have to stay with her. You do understand, don't you?'

Yes, she understood all right. She understood that Madame LeBlanc was a very strange, unpredictable, erratic woman.

'Is that why the shutters are all closed?'

Emil nodded.

'Maman insisted.'

He seemed confused, nervous. No wonder, having to deal with his mother's moods.

'Have you called a doctor?'

Emil stared at her.

'The local doctor is a fine man if you have a sprained ankle or a touch of influenza, but he can do nothing for my mother. I'm so sorry,' he said, putting out a hand to touch Sasha's arm.

'So you're trying to tell me I shan't be able to see you again?'

Her stomach muscles were clamping hard

inside her. She couldn't bear to go on living just across the road from Emil and not be able to see him.

'I want to be with you, Sasha, more than anything in the world. And we will be together, I promise you, but not this morning.'

He seemed to cheer up.

'Tonight the village of Saint Georges will hold a Pardon.'

'A what?'

Emil's smile was as warm and tender as ever.

'It's a sort of religious fête, held in church, but afterwards there is an open air event with dancing and a barbecue. Will you let me take you there, Sasha?'

'But what about your mother?'

'Her moods come and go,' he said simply.

Sasha had noticed that fact for herself.

'What causes them?' she asked. 'Was it something Mum and Dad or I did or said to upset her?'

Emil shook his head swiftly.

'Oh, no, no, you mustn't blame yourself. Look, I must go now. Shall I call for you tonight? About eight? If Maman is still ... Well, I will give her a sedative and put her to bed. She will sleep soundly till morning. Please, Sasha, don't be angry with me. I must see you again. It means so much to me.'

And to her. Sasha made up her mind quickly.

'All right. Call for me at eight.'

'I will.'

He kissed her cheek and scurried off into the house.

Sasha walked back to the cottage. She felt uneasy. Things didn't seem right, and how was she going to explain the change in her plans to her parents? She may as well go to Vannes with them now.

No word of criticism came from Anne, however, when Sasha returned to say she wouldn't be seeing Emil that morning. Anne did ask why and Sasha said as casually as she could, 'Oh, his mother is a bit off colour this morning.'

'Oh, what a shame!' Anne commiserated. 'Should I go round there, do you think?'

'No! I think she's resting in bed. By the way, Emil's calling round for me tonight. There's a barbecue and a dance in a nearby village. It should be fun.'

Her mother said nothing to that and went to get her bag prior to the trip to Vannes.

*　　*　　*

If Emil and Louise LeBlanc had not been so much on Sasha's mind she would have really enjoyed the outing, but wherever they went, whatever they did, the LeBlancs were in her thoughts. The large aquarium was interesting and the day culminated with a walk through the pine forests that bordered the impressive coastline. Before they came home they called in at a supermarket to buy fresh provisions.

Sasha was ready and waiting well before eight o'clock and then could only sit and bide her time. What if Emil didn't come? What if his mother wasn't well enough to be left? These and other anxious questions went through Sasha's mind.

Her parents had eaten their evening meal and by then Sasha was starving, so she stayed in her bedroom, looking wistfully out of the window till at last she saw Emil coming down the drive.

The sense of relief that shot through her was so strong that she almost lost the use of her legs. She darted away from the window and sank on to the edge of the bed and didn't move till she heard the anticipated knock on the door, whereupon she was propelled into immediate action and clattered down the stairs, reaching the door at the same time as her mother.

Emil stood on the doorstep. Tonight he wore light coloured trousers and a short-sleeved black shirt, open at the neck. He quite simply took Sasha's breath away.

'Good evening, Madame Hilton, Sasha,' he said with formal politeness.

'Good evening, Emil,' Anne returned before Sasha could find her voice. 'May I ask how you intend getting to this barbecue?'

Emil smiled at her.

'We shall go in my car, and don't worry, madame, I shall not keep Sasha out too late.'

'How is your mother?'

Sasha maintained her own silence.

'Much better, thank you. In fact she wishes me to apologise to Sasha for being indisposed this morning.'

'That's all right,' Sasha said shyly.

So once again Louise's mood had changed. Sasha decided to let sleeping dogs lie and not to mention Emil's mother unless he himself did so. If only her own mother would let them leave or at least ask Emil in for a drink or something, but she continued to stand in the open doorway and Sasha knew there was more to come.

'You realise, of course,' Anne began, 'that Sasha is a very young girl.'

'Mother,' Sasha mumbled under her breath, feeling hot and embarrassed.

Emil did not turn a hair.

'I realise she is young, madame,' he said. 'I can assure you that I will take the greatest care of your daughter and that I know perfectly well how to behave myself.'

This remark seemed to take Anne aback.

'I'm sure you do, Emil,' she said.

'Mum, can we go now?' Sasha pleaded.

Her mother looked at her.

'Of course. Have a good time,' and she reached forward and kissed Sasha's cheek.

'We'll leave the front door unlocked if we go to bed before you come back.'

At last they were free to go, but Sasha was aware that her mother was still standing in the doorway as she and Emil crossed the road towards Aux Camelias. As they stepped inside the gates, and were thus out of view of the cottage, Emil took hold of Sasha's hand.

'Did I pass the test?' he asked.

She looked at him and saw that he was teasing. She started to laugh.

'I'm sorry about that, but you know what mothers are.'

'Well, my mother has her faults, goodness knows, but she is delighted that I am seeing you tonight.'

Sasha was very unsure of that.

'Really?' she asked.

'Really. Please, you must not think that my mother's strange moods have anything to do with you, Sasha. They have not and she is perfectly all right now. Anyway, enough of parents for tonight. Let us just think of ourselves.'

Sasha was more than happy to agree to that. And that was the beginning. For the rest of the evening Sasha's feet did not touch the ground. She and Emil danced in the tiny square of the village. The music was provided by a three-piece band—two fiddlers and an accordionist, very French, very catchy, and people must have flocked to Saint Georges from miles around because the square was packed.

There was a makeshift bar underneath an awning and the barbecue itself with its acrid smell of burning charcoal and the hiss of grilling sausages and burgers and fried onions. Sasha declined Emil's offer of wine.

'Just a soft drink for me,' she said. 'I think I drank my year's quota of wine at your house last night.'

But Sasha didn't need the headiness of wine to lose herself completely in Emil's arms, resting her face against his chest, feeling his hand warm against her back. When the music became too quick and bouncy for them, they retired to the edge of the square to watch the others. Sasha loved it all. She had never been as happy. Then, she saw a small dark shape fluttering above, darting and weaving amongst the trees.

'What's that?' she asked Emil.

Emil laughed.

'Those are bats,' he told her.

'Bats!'

Sasha shuddered and turned her face in horror against Emil's shoulder.

Emil put his finger beneath Sasha's chin and lifted up her face. He was smiling gently.

'I would never let anything hurt you, Sasha,' he promised softly.

Then he was kissing her and they stood locked in each other's arms and it was just how Sasha had imagined it would be. She had been kissed before, not often it was true, for she hadn't had many boyfriends, but never like that. And because she wasn't the sort of girl who gave her kisses lightly, she knew in her heart how special Emil was to her, how special he had made her feel at the moment his lips met hers.

He released her mouth but kept his arms around her.

'Sasha, my petite,' he whispered so tenderly.

He seemed overwhelmed, unsure of himself.

'I am not sorry I did that.'

'I don't want you to be sorry, Emil,' Sasha told him.

He pushed a stray curl on her forehead.

'We must be sensible,' he warned.

'Yes, mustn't we?' she returned with a smile.

'We have only just met.'

'I know.'

'We must not allow our hearts to rule our heads.'

'Definitely not.'

Sasha didn't care. She only knew she never wanted to be parted from Emil again. How did he feel about her?

'It would be so easy to fall in love with you, Sasha.'

She reached up and put her hands on either side of his face, feeling its smooth, warm planes.

'I think I have already fallen in love with

you, Emil,' she told him.

* * *

They became inseparable after that night, and Sasha seemed to spend more time at Aux Camelias than she did at the cottage, because, miraculously, when Louise recovered from her sickness, she never slid back. Emil had only one word of caution for Sasha.

'Please don't speak of Paris to Maman,' he said.

It was a simple request and one with which Sasha was happy to comply and she pushed out of her mind the question. There was only one more moment of strain. Two days after the barbecue, her mother said, 'Now what about this return visit of Madame LeBlanc and Emil? I've been thinking.'

Anne's voice was full of enthusiasm as she went on. She did not yet know about the intensity of Sasha's and Emil's feelings for one another, and had obviously been giving the idea of preparing a dinner of her own some thought but Sasha, knowing that she and Emil had discussed this very subject was compelled to break in.

'They won't be coming, Mum,' she said.

Anne stared at her in surprise.

'Won't be coming? How do you know? I haven't asked them yet.'

'Madame LeBlanc never leaves the house,'

Sasha explained.

'What? Never?'

'Well, hardly ever. And then only in Emil's car.'

'She must be agoraphobic,' Anne stated.

Sasha had never thought of that. It would explain some of Louise's strange behaviour if not all of it. Sasha could see her mother was a bit disgruntled but said nothing, believing the subject was closed, but later, Anne brought it up again.

'Is that why Emil doesn't work?'

'Pardon?'

At first Sasha did not know what her mother was talking about.

'Because his mother has a phobia. It could be the reason, I suppose. Ah, well, it's none of our business.'

Anne dismissed the matter with a shrug of her shoulders and went out to sit with John in the enclosed garden. Sasha watched them through the kitchen window. Before long she would be meeting Emil, and being with him was now the most important thing in her life.

She knew she was going to have to tell her parents sooner or later, how she and Emil felt about one another, but she didn't know how to put it into words. Time seemed to be going by so quickly. Sasha tried not to dwell on that, but she couldn't help it. How could she go back to England and leave Emil? It didn't bear thinking about.

It wasn't long before Sasha's mother seemed to see the light as far as Sasha and Emil were concerned. Her father was a different matter. He wouldn't notice the certain glow that seemed to surround his daughter these days, nor think anything unusual about a boy and girl wanting to spend all their time together. Not in a month of Sundays. But Anne was different.

When Sasha returned from Aux Camelias late one night, Anne was waiting up for her.

'Mum, you shouldn't have waited up for me,' Sasha said.

'Well, if I didn't, I wouldn't see much of you these days, would I?'

Sasha came and sat by her mother on the couch.

'That's not true,' she said defensively.

Anne didn't argue the point. Instead she asked, 'Is it serious?'

Sasha nodded. There was a pause before Anne went on.

'Oh, Sasha, I don't want to be a killjoy but do you think it's wise to spend so much time alone with Emil?'

'We're not doing anything wrong,' Sasha said defiantly.

Anne patted her daughter's hand.

'I didn't think for one minute that you were, but don't you realise how difficult you'll make things for yourselves when our holiday is over and we have to go home?'

'We've talked about that, Mum. We shall write to one another. And as soon as he can, Emil will come over to England. It isn't just a holiday romance, Mum.'

'Darling,' Anne began, 'you're so young. And what about Emil? He doesn't appear to work at all, so . . .'

Sasha broke in angrily.

'Emil says I've got nothing to worry about, financial or otherwise.'

'And you believe him?'

'Yes, I believe him. Why shouldn't I?'

'Don't shout, darling,' Anne reproved.

Sasha found that she was trembling. Arguments with either of her parents were rare events in her life. They usually got on so well, but then she realised that her mother and father had always approved of what she did, where she went and whom she saw. In fact, Sasha thought wryly, she had been the perfect daughter, never giving her parents cause for distress or disharmony.

But she had to make them see now that she and Emil were not going to give one another up. They were in love. Sasha knew what she was doing. Surely because of her complete lack of casual relationships, as most of her friends had already experienced by now, Anne must see how serious she was about Emil.

'Sasha, you're my baby, my little girl. No, don't interrupt, please, let me finish. Because we only had the one child, you're doubly precious to us. I know one day you'll leave us and make your own way in the world, but . . .'

She paused.

Sasha smiled in spite of her inner turmoil.

'But you'd rather it wasn't just yet.'

Anne smiled, too, and some of the tension between them began to disperse.

'I suppose so,' she admitted.

'Mum, you don't have to worry. I'm going to be fine. I love Emil. He loves me. Oh, much of what you say is true. We are both young and we live hundreds of miles apart. We've known each other just a few weeks, but I know, Mum. There isn't a doubt in my mind, and we're not getting married next week, you know!'

She could see by the expression on her mother's face that she had said the wrong thing.

'Married? You've discussed marriage?'

Sasha looked down at her hands.

'Well, yes, we have,' she murmured.

'Oh, Sasha!'

There was such pain, such horror in those two short words that Sasha felt their moment of closeness could never again be achieved. Because of her hurt, she flared into anger, pulling away from her mother, going to the fireplace, staring at the cooling, crumbling ashes.

'Mum, you haven't listened to me at all, have you?' she cried. 'What do you think we intend to do? Become merely penfriends?

That's what you'd like, isn't it? So you can live in hope that it'll all fizzle out one day. But it isn't going to be like that.'

She swung round to face Anne.

'We love one another. How many times do I have to say it? Have some faith in me, Mum. Don't you know me at all?'

Anne stood up, too, and tried to reach out for Sasha but she jerked away from the outstretched hand.

'I want you to like Emil, Mum,' Sasha said. 'I want you to be kind and welcoming to him. He'll be your son-in-law one day. We've always been such a close-knit family. Don't let's drift apart at the most important time of my life.'

Impulsively she kissed her mother's cheek then without another word she left the room and went up to bed.

CHAPTER SIX

The weather turned cool soon after they got home again. Was it so in Brittany, Sasha asked herself, or were they still enjoying the hot sunshine? Emil was constantly in her thoughts. Now they had to keep in touch by letter. They wrote to each other every day and it seemed to Sasha that their love for one another grew stronger.

Sasha started a job at the public library,

working in the reference section. She quickly made new friends and still saw many of her old ones, but she rarely went out. She had never been a one for clubs and pubs. Now she became a veritable homebird, living for her work and Emil's letters.

It was towards the middle of October when the package arrived. It was there on the hall table when Sasha came home in the evening. She recognised the postmark and Emil's writing at once. She hung up her coat and took the package into the kitchen where her mother, as usual, was putting the finishing touches to the evening meal.

'I wonder what this is,' she said, feeling excited.

How sweet of Emil to send her some little gift, the first she had ever received from him. Whatever it was she would treasure it for ever.

'Best open it, then you'll know,' her mother said.

Since their return from Brittany, Sasha had regained her normal, easy relationship with her mother. When Emil's daily letter came, Anne always asked after him and his mother and sometimes Sasha shared little snippets of information with both her parents. Sometimes Sasha couldn't help wondering if her mother believed Emil was less of a threat now that he was on the other side of the Channel. Out of sight, out of mind perhaps. If so, she couldn't be more wrong.

'I see the parcel is registered,' Sasha remarked, turning it over in her hand. 'It must be valuable or important.'

'Yes,' Anne said, 'I had to sign for it.'

'I think I'll take it upstairs, if you don't mind, Mum,' Sasha said.

'Of course.'

In her bedroom, Sasha placed Emil's parcel on her dressing table and sat staring at it for several seconds. Why was she so reluctant to open it? It wasn't as though she thought the contents would be something horrible, something she wouldn't like. She trusted Emil implicitly. It was just that her mind was beginning to run away with fantastic notions and once that had happened she knew how disappointed she would be if she was wrong.

Of course, she was wrong! She pulled herself together sharply, using her nail scissors to cut away the sticky tape that bound the package. It wouldn't happen this way. They had talked about marriage, yes, but Emil had never asked her formally and though Sasha knew if he had, her answer would have been yes, she would have to be patient and wait till they could meet. She was already hoping for a Christmas reunion. She had dreamed often of the occasion when Emil would place a ring on her finger, a ring chosen together.

She tore away the brown wrapping paper and the layers of inner tissue paper. There was a folded sheet of white notepaper—Emil's letter. Sasha picked it up. Oh, my goodness! There was no disguising the ring box, dark green velvet, smooth and warm in her hands. With held breath she opened it up. The ring nestled in the green satin lining, a square emerald surrounded by small sparkling diamonds. She didn't remove it. Instead she opened up Emil's letter.

My Darling Sasha,
Forgive my unorthodox manner of asking you to do me the honour of becoming my wife, but I simply could not wait till I held you in my arms to know that you are truly mine, for ever. I am sorry but I won't be able to come to England for some time yet and I wanted you to have no doubts as to my love for you. This ring was my grandmother's given to her by my grandfather upon their engagement.
It is a family heirloom, always handed down the male line to be used on a betrothal. As my mother had no brothers or sisters, the ring came to me. Sasha, my love, you would do me the greatest honour in the world if you would wear this ring. Of course, if you would prefer a new ring, one of your very own, I will understand.

Sasha took the ring from its box and slipped it on her wedding finger. It fitted her perfectly. Had Emil had its size altered to fit her? And how had he known the size of her finger? She couldn't stop the happy tears from springing to her eyes. The ring was beautiful. She would never have wanted any other. She went back to Emil's letter.

I had the ring reduced in size a little. I hope it fits. Your hands are so delicate, such slender fingers.

Emil went on paying her compliments, saying how much he loved her, how greatly he missed her. She wished he could be there, but it was not to be and she knew there must be a very good reason for this. She stared at her ring, giving a little shudder when she considered the risk Emil had taken sending it through the post, even though it had been registered. But she had received it safely and would wear it with love and pride.

She went back downstairs, eager to show the ring to her mother but at the same time fearing her reaction now that she and Emil were officially engaged. Anne was setting the table in the dining-room. As Sasha hesitated in the doorway, the front door opened and John came in.

'Hello, Dad,' Sasha greeted.

'Hi, love.' John sniffed the air appreciatively. 'Something smells good!'

Awkwardly Sasha held out her left hand.

'Look,' she stated, feeling she was going

about announcing her engagement completely the wrong way but not knowing how else to do it.

John stepped forward undoing his coat.

'My word!' he said in a stunned voice.

'What's the matter?'

Anne came out of the dining-room, carrying an empty tray. John looked at his wife.

'Seems like our little girl has got herself engaged,' he said.

'What!'

Anne dropped the tray on the hall table and snatched up Sasha's hand, staring at the ring as though she couldn't believe her eyes.

'So that's what your parcel contained. You've been expecting this, haven't you? That's why you were so eager to open the parcel in private.'

Sasha was too shocked to answer but her father said, in a voice that held a note of reproach, 'Hey, come on, Anne, that's no way to behave. Aren't you going to kiss Sasha, to congratulate her? I am.'

He took his daughter in his arms.

'My very best wishes to you both. He's a grand young man.'

'Thank you, Dad,' Sasha said gratefully.

'And a bit of a romantic, I'd guess,' John teased, 'proposing by post. Good for him!'

Anne stared at him.

'You mean you don't mind?' she asked.

'Why should I mind? To tell you the truth I

saw it coming. Oh, I know they're both young, but I know they're going to be sensible about this. There's no rush to go down the aisle, is there?'

He smiled at Sasha. She smiled nervously in return, saying nothing. She knew neither she nor Emil would want a long engagement. In fact she was going to write and suggest a Christmas wedding. She would go to live in Brittany, of course, maybe with Louise at Aux Camelias to begin with till they got their own place. In fact they had already made plans, oh, nothing definitely decided upon, but they both knew what they wanted, so why pretend they didn't?

Anne turned to her daughter.

'Sasha,' she began, 'I want you to promise me one thing. I want you to invite Emil to stay with us. He can come for as long as he likes. Let me have a proper chance to get to know him. Your father, too, though it seems he's been won over to having a French son-in-law already. Well, maybe I'm a bit more conservative. Maybe I don't want you to do something you may spend the rest of your life regretting.'

She smiled suddenly and gave Sasha a kiss.

'I only want your happiness, darling. Please believe that.'

'I do, Mum, I do.'

Sasha hugged her mother.

CHAPTER SEVEN

Time passed rapidly after the engagement but still Emil had not put in an appearance. His letters were full of apologies. He constantly urged Sasha to go ahead with the arrangements for the wedding.

'I'll be there,' he promised her. 'I know I have to establish residency in England before we marry and there's no way I'm going to jeopardise that.'

He sent her money to make various arrangements, which Anne said they didn't need. Sasha slipped it into the cover of her building society passbook. Now, rows and friction were more or less constant between Sasha and her mother.

'This is ridiculous, Sasha,' Anne said. 'What's he playing at?'

'He can't help it, Mum,' Sasha insisted. 'I know he has his reasons for not coming.'

'What reasons, for heaven's sake?'

Sasha couldn't answer except to say, 'He'll be here.' But sometimes even she felt full of doubts. This wasn't the way it should be. They were supposed to be together, seeing to all the wedding plans, listening to the banns being read, supervising the sending out of invitations. Sasha felt she was continually explaining away Emil's absence, her excuses beginning to sound feeble in her own ears. Sometimes she saw sympathy on people's faces. That she could not bear.

The worry began to make her feel ill. She wasn't sleeping well, felt tired all the time, drained of energy. But she held her head high and didn't let her parents see how low she felt. If she gave in to her despair she knew Anne would have won.

Whenever a letter came from Emil—he was writing only about once a week now—his declarations of undying love, his complete faith that he would soon be with her, renewed her hope and kept her going. Then the letters ceased all together. Every evening when she came home from work she would say, 'Nothing today, Mum?'

'No, I'm sorry.'

There was sympathy now in Anne's voice. Sasha knew her mother felt her pain and frustration, but this only made matters worse because Sasha felt what Anne really wanted to say was, 'I told you so.'

Sasha's lack of proper sleep continued to make her feel run down and depressed. She couldn't concentrate at work. When Anne made what she intended to be a helpful suggestion, saying, 'Can't you phone Emil? Surely it would be better to hear what he has to say, rather than go through all this worry and uncertainty,' Sasha almost bit her mother's head off.

'I can't phone him, Mum. Don't you think if it was that simple I'd do it? There is no phone at Aux Camelias.'

Quietly Anne asked, 'Couldn't he phone you from a callbox if for some reason he hasn't been able to write?'

Sasha, without answering, ran up to her room and indulged in one of her now frequent bouts of weeping. Of course Emil could phone. She had given him her number ages ago. That he had chosen not to do so was a complete mystery to her.

The next day, Sasha collapsed at work and her supervisor immediately called an ambulance. After various tests she was diagnosed as suffering from glandular fever and it was to be a very long time before she felt well enough to start fighting back and to become determined to find out just what had happened to Emil.

CHAPTER EIGHT

The weather was so different from Sasha's last visit to Brittany but at least there was no snow. The crossing from Portsmouth to Saint Malo had been rather rough, but Sasha was a good sailor and had spent part of the time on deck, in the early morning as it was coming light, braving the cold wind, watching the grey, churning waves.

At Saint Malo, feeling like a seasoned traveller, she had driven her car effortlessly through the Breton countryside, finally reaching Pontivy early afternoon, tired but resolute after her long journey from the north of England. From then it was only a short journey to Melrand and hence to Aux Camelias.

This time she drove straight through the open gates, taking in the bare trees, the lawn with its covering of white frost. Today no bright flowers bloomed, no green foliage adorned the trees. But the house itself had not changed and, as she climbed out of the car, Sasha felt the tightening of her stomach as the first really nervous feeling since leaving home descended on her.

There would be no Emil to greet her, she knew that, and no Emilie Couriol either, but Sophie would be there, kind-hearted Sophie who had asked her to come here. On her previous visit, Sasha had felt that Sophie Couriol had wanted to say so much more than she had done. Only the presence of her older sister had held her back. Now Emilie was dead. There would be just the two of them.

Sasha knew that for the first time there was real hope. Would she soon be meeting Emil? Would the time they had been apart fade into insignificance as he took her in his arms? She could forgive him anything, no matter what it was, if only she could believe that soon they would be man and wife and never again be parted.

Before she could ring the doorbell, the door was opened by Sophie. There was a wide smile of welcome on her face as she ushered Sasha inside. The warmth of the house immediately embraced her.

'Mademoiselle,' Sophie exclaimed, 'how good it is to see you!'

Sasha put down her small suitcase.

'Won't you call me Sasha?' she suggested. 'I feel we are friends.'

'Yes, we are,' Sophie agreed. 'So you must call me Sophie. Is this case all your luggage?' she said in a rather disappointed voice. 'I thought you might stay with me for some time.'

Sasha wondered if Sophie was lonely now that her elder sister, with whom she had probably spent a great deal, if not all, of her life, was dead.

'It's very kind of you to invite me here,' Sasha said, 'but I'm hoping what you have to tell me will mean I shall soon be seeing Emil again.'

Sophie's smile was understanding.

'I hope so, too,' she said, 'but first you must go to your room and freshen up.'

She led the way upstairs.

'I will make some coffee. Then we can talk.'

'But you do know where Emil is?' Sasha

persisted.

Sophie paused halfway up the stairs, putting her veined hand over Sasha's own.

'I know where he is, Sasha,' she said, 'but you must be patient. You have waited so long. What do a few more minutes mean?'

Was she really as close as that to knowing Emil's whereabouts? Sasha tried desperately to rein in her excitement, but she was starting to tremble and to feel that she could scarcely breathe. She tried not to let Sophie see how her emotions were running riot.

Sophie showed her into a small, cosy room at the top of the stairs. Sasha had never been upstairs before. There had been no need to, not even to use the bathroom as there was a cloakroom leading off the downstairs hall, but she was not disappointed.

The room was furnished in the same solid, rather old-fashioned style as the downstairs rooms. There was a high bed covered with a white duvet, a dressing table and wardrobe and near the window, outside of which the last of the pale wintry sunshine was fast fading, was a winged arm chair covered with rose pink velvet. Matching curtains hung at the window from a wooden pole with large brass rings. The room was warm and Sasha saw the modern electric heater under the window.

'Voila!' Sophie declared. 'I think you will find this a pleasant room. The bathroom is two doors away down the hall.'

Later, when Sasha went back downstairs and entered the familiar drawing-room where a crackling log fire was burning in the hearth and the heavy curtains had been drawn across the windows, she came to realise at once that Sophie held no doubts and suspicions about her.

Before the Frenchwoman poured out the coffee, she took her place in the chair where Sasha remembered Emilie Couriol sitting, where she had first become aware of the older sister's lack of sight, and beckoned Sasha towards her.

'Show me your ring,' she said, and Sasha held out her left hand.

Sophie took hold of it and smoothed a long finger over the emerald.

'So beautiful!' she murmured.

'Yes, isn't it? It belonged to Emil's grandmother. A family heirloom he told me.'

Sophie looked at her, still holding her hand.

'Did Emil give you the ring whilst you were in Brittany?'

'No. He sent it to me.'

'I see. Please, sit down.'

Sasha did so, wondering why Sophie was so interested in the ring. Sophie picked up the coffee pot.

'I knew you were speaking the truth the moment you showed me your ring when you were here in July.'

She spoke slowly, matching her actions to

her words, pouring out the coffee.

'I recognised it. You see, Emil LeBlanc's grandmother was the sister-in-law of Emilie and myself, being the wife of our only brother, Michel, who was, of course, Louise's father.'

Sasha gasped.

'So Emil and Louise weren't just two people who leased your house?' she asked.

'No. I am Louise's aunt and Emil's great aunt.'

Sophie passed Sasha her coffee which she took and lowered immediately on to the coffee table in front of her. She wanted neither to eat nor drink until the mystery was finally unravelled.

Sophie went on, 'Do you not now wonder why Emilie did not challenge you about the ring? I was wise enough to keep quiet about it at the time, but my sister, well, you do not need me to tell you that she was a forthright, outspoken person.'

Sasha looked into Sophie's kind blue eyes.

'But your sister was blind.'

It was a statement not a question.

'Yes, she was, but how did you guess?'

'I don't know. I suppose the dark glasses helped, but there were some little gestures that also gave it away, but,' she hastened to add, 'your sister was very capable.'

Sophie gave a little laugh.

'Oh, she was,' she agreed, 'she certainly was,' but there was kindness not hostility in her voice. 'She became blind as a child of eight. Complications after measles, I'm afraid, but she always insisted on being independent. We lived together through mutual need, companionship, not because of Emilie's disability.

'She never thought of it as a disability and wouldn't allow anyone else to do so either. Emilie loved to travel. She enjoyed our many trips to many different countries. She often said she could smell the fresh air, feel the sunshine, listen to voices, the running of rivers, the chime of church bells. Her enjoyment of everything around her was not impaired by her lack of vision. When she discovered she had a terminal illness, that, too, she took in her stride and we took off for Scandinavia.'

Sophie paused and Sasha waited politely, but wished her hostess would begin to talk about Emil. She didn't want to be rude or indifferent, but she hadn't come all this way to listen to stories of Sophie's late sister, interesting, uplifting though those may be. Then Sophie began again, replacing her own cup carefully in its saucer.

'Just before we went to Scandinavia, we received a letter from Louise. She asked if she and Emil could come and stay with us. They lived in Paris and we had not seen them for quite some time. As there appeared to be a sense of urgency in our niece's letter, I took it upon myself to phone her at her Paris home.

'I went into Melrand and used the public phone. Louise was very distressed and said she and Emil had to get away from Paris. I had to tell her that Emilie and I were going on holiday in less than a week, and that Aux Camelias would be empty for several months.

'Louise suggested she and Emil come here and take over the house whilst we were away. Naturally, I willingly agreed. I arranged to leave the keys at the bakery and that was that. Emilie was in full agreement with what I had done.'

'But why couldn't Emilie have told me that in the first place?' Sasha asked. 'Why pretend she hardly knew Louise and Emil?'

Sophie stared at her.

'She had her reasons.'

'And you still don't intend to tell me what those reasons were?'

'What I will tell you, Sasha, is that I know Emilie was quite wrong about you. She mistrusted you, whereas I had a strong belief in you. But in defence of my sister, I must say that she was only thinking of Louise and her son, who, incidentally is our godson as well as our great nephew.'

Sasha, instead of becoming enlightened by what was being said, was growing more confused.

'You said earlier that Louise was very distressed when she asked if she could come here. Did she tell you why?'

'She did.'

One thing at least was clearer to understand now. Louise's strange, erratic behaviour, the fear she had displayed at the mention of Paris, even the day of the closed shutters could be explained. At the meal the evening before, Louise had talked about Paris and her life there with affection. The next morning, Emil had asked that Paris not be mentioned to his mother. What had happened in the capital?

'And this distress was in some way responsible for Emil's deserting me?' Sasha asked.

'Yes, it was,' Sophie answered, 'and I will tell you now, Sasha, what it is you really want to know. Emil's whereabouts.'

Sasha sat on the edge of the couch gripping the cushions with tight fingers. She didn't speak. She couldn't, and she could feel her heart beating so fast and so loudly it seemed it would burst right out of her throat.

'He wrote to us from Switzerland, Lucerne, exactly. He explained he had taken his mother there, that she was very ill and in a clinic.'

'Switzerland!' Sasha repeated. 'Why there?'

Sophie shrugged.

'Who knows? I gather that Emil believed it was safe there.'

Sasha frowned.

'Safe? Was he in trouble, in danger?'

Sophie smiled.

'Safe for Louise. Emil spoke highly of the

Lucerne clinic.'

Sasha felt compelled to ask, 'Is this clinic a hospital for the sick, or is it an establishment for the mentally ill?'

Sophie gave her a strange look.

'What makes you ask that, Sasha?' she queried.

Sasha told her about her suspicions regarding Louise's odd behaviour. Sophie nodded.

'You are right. Louise was—how can I put it without sounding terribly cruel? She was unwell in her mind. But believe me, she had cause to be.'

She paused and a silence fell between them, broken only by the crackling of the logs in the hearth and the hypnotic ticking of a clock.

'Yes?'

Sasha could hardly bear the suspense. Why was Sophie intent on torturing her? Why was the story taking so long to unfold?

'I cannot go into those reasons, my dear. Those are for Emil himself to explain, if he so chooses.'

Sasha felt a sudden surge of anger.

'But you must tell me! You must!' she cried. 'You asked me to come here. You must know why Emil chose not to write to me any more. We were to have been married at Christmas. He was writing to me nearly every day, as I was to him, then suddenly there were no more letters, only silence. After that I was ill myself for some time before I came here in the summer. Then you wrote to me, and here I am. Well, my trip hasn't done me much good, has it? Can you imagine how happy I was when I received your letter? What a tremendous sense of relief, of hope I felt?'

Suddenly she was sobbing, covering her face with her hands. As she sobbed, she became aware that Sophie was sitting by her on the couch, an arm around her shoulders, holding her close. She felt comforted and in a strange way, safe in Sophie's arms.

'You are upset, ma petite,' the Frenchwoman said softly. 'But you must understand that I cannot tell you more than I have to. There are deep family problems involved.'

Sasha looked up through a haze of tears.

'Is Emil already married?'

Sophie laughed.

'Good heavens, no, nothing like that. He gave you his grandmother's ring. What more proof do you need of his love for you?'

'So, whatever those family problems are, you believe eventually all will be well between Emil and me? You think, despite all the signs to the contrary, that he never meant to hurt me, that when I eventually meet him he will be able to explain his long silence in a way that I will understand?'

'Isn't that what you have always believed yourself, Sasha? In your heart?'

It was true. She had. Against all odds she had kept faith with Emil's promise to marry her. She gave a weak smile.

'I have never doubted Emil's love,' she said.

'And nor do I,' Sophie said. 'It's true, my nephew didn't speak of you when he wrote to us from Switzerland, but he was in turmoil. His mother was his only concern at that time. You must go to him, I'm certain of that. Otherwise I wouldn't be telling you all this. And I'd like to tell you another story, if I may. It concerns myself, and something that happened just before the war when I was about your age.

'I fell in love, just as you did with Emil. We didn't become engaged, didn't have the opportunity for that. Mine was a rich, influential banking family, you understand, and when my brother, Michel, became engaged to a lovely girl from a similar background, naturally they had our parents' blessing. Because of Emilie's blindness, there was no great hope she would ever marry. Today such an affliction would not be a bar to matrimony, but in those days, well, things were very different.'

She paused and Sasha waited for her to continue, momentarily putting thoughts of Emil aside, captivated by what Sophie Couriol was telling her. Sophie went on, her hands folded neatly now in her lap.

'I met Jacques in the park, of all places, and there was an instant attraction between us. I don't know why, perhaps because he made me laugh, or perhaps because he had the friendliest of brown eyes.'

She could be talking about Emil, Sasha thought.

'However, Jacques came from a humble background. He was a clerk in a firm of lawyers. He lived with his widowed mother in a poor part of Paris. I invited him home to meet my parents. On that one and only occasion he took tea with us, Maman and Papa could not have been more gracious had he been of royal blood, but after he left they made it very plain to me that I must never see Jacques again. Of course, I disobeyed them. I went to meet Jacques' mother. She loved and treated me like a daughter. But, I was found out. You don't want to know, my dear, how my parents reacted, how they treated me, the terrible way they dealt with Madame Delon, Jacques' mother.

'Suffice it to say that I was given an ultimatum. I could have my Jacques and live my life in poverty, or I could remain a part of the Couriol family. I could not have both. If I chose the former, I would have to leave the family home without luggage, without a penny to my name. I would have to leave that same day.'

Sophie gave a long, weary sigh.

'I was weak. I was used to comfort and riches. I was scared to think I could never see my dear papa and maman or my brother and sister ever again. And there was by then a general unrest throughout Europe. I feared for the future. I capitulated. I never saw Jacques again. But I never married. At least I stood firm on that count.'

Sophie seemed to give herself a brisk, mental shake. She turned to Sasha.

'Perhaps my story does not compare with yours in any way,' she said, 'because you have your parents' blessing, but I've told it to you to show you that you must go on, you must never give in. Whatever you have to face when you get to Lucerne, whatever you learn about Emil and his mother, remember how much you love one another.'

Sasha gave Sophie a warm, impulsive hug.

'I will, oh, I will!' she cried with a great uplifting of her heart.

CHAPTER NINE

To give Anne credit, she did try to hide her dismay and concern that when Sasha came home she was planning yet another trip abroad. But she made it plain that she was merely worried about her daughter's health.

'Couldn't you wait at least until the weather improves?' she suggested. 'Spring perhaps? That isn't so far away. I'm sure all this dashing here, there and everywhere can't be doing you any good.'

Sasha smiled patiently.

'I'm fine, Mum,' she said, though in truth she was feeling tired, washed out, despite being buoyed up by her determination to reach Emil as soon as possible. 'Don't worry about me.'

Anne frowned.

'And what about your work?'

Sasha looked down at the travellers' cheques she was busy looking over in preparation for her departure for Switzerland.

'I've given up my job,' she said quietly.

'You've what?' her mother exclaimed.

Still not looking at her mother, Sasha went on, 'I thought it was only fair. I don't know how long it's going to take me to find Emil, or what will be the outcome when I do find him.'

'But I thought Sophie Couriol had given you his address.'

Sasha nodded.

'Yes, she has, or at least his last known address.'

'So you don't even know that this isn't going to be another wasted journey.'

Sasha closed the booklet of cheques firmly. She stood up and faced her mother.

'Even if it is, I've got to give it a go, Mum. But I couldn't, in all fairness, expect them to keep my job open. I wasn't due to much official holiday and what with my being ill as well. And, who knows, Emil and I might settle in Switzerland. You and Dad can come for holidays.'

She sounded flippant, she knew that, but she was determined to remain cheerful and optimistic. She could see her mother striving to keep her patience.

'And just how do you expect to support yourself whilst all this is going on?'

Sasha hesitated. It was true her meagre savings were dropping at an alarming rate. She had never been a big spender and had accrued some funds by banking birthday and Christmas money. She didn't know how long she would be away from home on this occasion and she wouldn't expect Emil to provide for her. She wasn't his wife yet.

'Well?' Anne prompted.

'I've got Grandma's money,' she said defiantly.

A couple of thousand pounds lay in an interest paying building society account. Sasha had intended saving the money towards the day when she finally left home and set up on her own. She had expected, as most of her friends had, to get a flat, to become independent. But she hadn't planned on meeting someone, of falling in love.

'So you'd squander Grandma's money, would you?' Anne's voice was a little sad.

'I wouldn't be squandering it!' Sasha protested. 'And I don't even know if I shall need it yet. Oh, Mum, what's happening to us? We never used to argue like this. You were my best friend. Is it because you're afraid of losing me? Do you think I'm going to go out of your lives for ever?'

She knew instantly by the expression in her mother's eyes that she had hit the nail on the head. She went on quietly, crossing to her mother's side.

'I'm right, aren't I? I'm still your baby and you don't want me to grow up and flee the nest. It won't be like that, Mum, I promise you. When I find Emil, when all the confusion, the hurt and, yes, the anger, has gone away, when Emil and I are married, you'll learn to love him as I do. He's a wonderful person, Mum. Wherever we decide to live, we shall see you and Dad as often as we can.'

She saw Anne's eyes mist over with tears. She reached out and took hold of her mother's hand, holding it tightly.

'I love you, Mum,' she vowed fervently.

Anne's lips trembled into a smile.

'I hope your Emil realises how lucky he is,' she said. 'I'm so proud of you, darling. Oh, I know I've tried to hinder you, put you off, but that's only because I love you so much. And you're right, I'm scared stiff of losing you. But then, even if you were only marrying the boy next door I should probably feel like that. Go to Emil, with my blessing and God go with you. You deserve all the luck you can get.'

* * *

Lucerne was a winter wonderland. Snow sparkled in the streets and the lakeside gardens, glistened on the surrounding mountains, white and brilliant in the clear, winter sunshine. Sasha had never been anywhere more beautiful. How she wished she and Emil were together here, perhaps on honeymoon in this lovely Alpine city. But they weren't.

First she had to go to the address that Sophie Couriol had given her. Eager as she was to do that, she had decided to wait till the day after her arrival, to get acquainted with her surroundings, to walk by the lake, to visit some of the shops and department stores—generally to see the sights just like any other tourist.

It may be odd of her to do that. After all, she had practically moved heaven and earth to find Emil, but now she really believed her search was almost at an end and deep down she was a little afraid, afraid of what she would say to him when they finally came face to face. Even more afraid of what he would have to say to her.

Sophie had been very cryptic, but Sasha knew there had been some deep problems to cause Emil to desert her as he had. Even allowing for the fact of Louise's obvious illness, couldn't he at the very least have got some word to her? He had always known her whereabouts but to her it was as though he had simply vanished into thin air. She shrugged off those disturbing thoughts.

The travel agent had arranged a booking for her at a central hotel, not far from the river. From a city map, Sasha judged that it was just a short walk to where Emil had an apartment.

She spent a quiet, restful afternoon. The air was crisp and cold and with the early setting of the sun became even colder. By then Sasha had returned to the hotel, there to eat an excellent dinner and retire early to bed. She lay in the high, comfortable bed, listening to the occasional passing car, but the traffic was light.

'Tomorrow,' she spoke aloud, 'God willing, Emil, darling, we'll be together again.'

CHAPTER TEN

It was a smart, elegant building, old and mellow, on a quiet residential street. Sasha's heart took a wild leap as she read the names beside the bell pushes. Emil LeBlanc occupied apartment number six on the first floor.

Would he be home? It was early morning. She had left the hotel immediately after breakfast and it had taken her only about fifteen minutes to walk here. But he could be out. He could be visiting his mother or doing some shopping.

Sasha braced her shoulders and pushed the appropriate bell. Within seconds a voice came over the intercom.

'Hello. C'est Emil LeBlanc.'

Sasha stepped back in mild shock. She had not expected to hear his voice so quickly and so clearly. She had thought perhaps a buzzer might sound, admitting her to the building. Then she would have gone up the stairs, or maybe used a lift, giving herself time to compose herself before knocking on Emil's apartment door. Now she had no option but to answer him.

'Emil, it's me, Sasha.'

Simple words, but what else could she say? There was a long pause. Then Emil's voice came again.

'Oh, mon Dieu! Sasha!'

Then at last, the expected buzzer sounded and Sasha pushed open the heavy, wooden door, finding herself in a large, tiled hall. The inside of the building was as elegant as the outside. Sasha started to climb the marble steps, not looking for a lift. She heard a door open above her, running footsteps and there he was, looking down at her, his eyes wide with surprise, his fingers gripping the banister.

His hair seemed longer, but he still had a lock of it flopping on to his forehead. Sasha started to run. They met on the landing and then they were in each other's arms and she was crying.

'Oh, Emil, Emil!' she sobbed. 'I've waited so long, so long for this moment. Why did you go away like that? How could you hurt me so much?'

'Sasha, my darling Sasha.'

Emil was kissing her eyes, her cheeks, her trembling lips.

'Come inside. Oh, I can't believe this is happening. How did you find me? What can I say? Can you forgive me? Can you ever forgive me?'

She knew she could forgive him anything. As Emil lead her into the warmth of his apartment where she took in nothing of her surroundings, Sasha believed nothing mattered now that she had found him at last. He still loved her. But he had to tell her his story, fill in the gaps left by his Great Aunt Sophie.

'Why did you stop writing, Emil?'

She came straight to the point, sitting down on a plush, deep red settee, fiddling with a button on her coat.

'We were to have been married, but you never came. Why didn't you write to me, Emil?'

He sat beside her, holding her hand, his eyes anxiously on hers, his expression searching, perhaps for signs of her understanding, and forgiveness. Well, he could have both, but she had to know the whole truth. Only then could they rebuild their lives together.

'It was Maman. I had to get her away from Brittany. It happened so fast. She became ill.'

Sasha nodded.

'Yes, I know that.'

'You do? How?' Emil looked puzzled.

'I went to Brittany in the summer. I met your Great Aunt Sophie and Emilie.'

'And they told you where I was?'

'No, not then. Your Great Aunt Emilie was very suspicious of me. She told me lies about you. She said you and your mother were merely tenants who had leased Aux Camelias, but I didn't believe her.'

'Then?' Emil prompted gently.

'Much later I had a letter from Sophie Couriol telling me that Emilie was dead, saying she knew I had been speaking the truth when I said I was your fiancée, asking me to visit Aux Camelias again. So I did. And here I am. And now, Emil, don't you think you should be explaining things to me?'

Emil's smile was tremulous.

'Of course, I will do that, but first, just one or two more questions. And please, let me take your coat. Would you like some coffee or hot chocolate perhaps?'

Sasha shook her head.

'No, nothing, thanks. I've only recently had breakfast.'

She stood up whilst Emil helped her off with her coat. His hands lingered on her shoulders.

'You are as beautiful as ever,' he murmured.

He moved as though to kiss her, but she pulled away.

'No, Emil, we must talk. We must.'

She had to be firm, though she yearned to be in the warmth and safety of his arms.

'Yes, of course.'

They sat down again.

'What made my Great Aunt Sophie believe in you, Sasha?'

Sasha held out her left hand.

'This,' she said.

Emil stared at the ring.

'You still wear it?'

'Shouldn't I? Doesn't it mean anything any more?'

A hurt look flashed into his brown eyes.

'I hope so, but that will be for you to decide when I tell you what happened.'

So Emil talked and Sasha listened and she allowed him to hold her hand, because even such brief contact gave them a deep awareness of each other, a comfort which they both desperately needed.

'I suppose I must begin at the beginning,' Emil said, 'so that you will know how everything started. It may take me some time.'

'I have all the time in the world,' Sasha assured him.

Emil went on, 'I suppose my Great Aunt

told you something about our family.'

Sasha nodded.

'Yes. She said you were in the banking business.'

'That's right. Generations of Couriols have dealt in commerce and banking, and generally whenever someone from the family marries it is to a person from the same sort of background.'

Sasha remembered Sophie's story of Jacques Delon. She was also aware that she herself did not come from that sort of background. She said nothing.

'My mother broke that trend. She went against her family's wishes and married what I am sure my relatives thought of as an outsider. He had not a penny to his name. He purported to be a writer, but I don't think he ever had anything published. His name was Phillipe LeBlanc, my own father, of course, and he was most charming and very handsome.'

Did Emil favour his father at all, Sasha found herself wondering, in looks, that is.

'My mother, as you saw for yourself, is a very beautiful woman, and when she was younger, she was quite stunning. She was also very rich, a perfect target for a man like my father.'

So there was no love lost there. Sasha wondered how Phillipe LeBlanc fitted into the mystery. Well, no doubt she would soon find out.

'They married, against the family wishes, but to be fair my father was given every opportunity to better himself. He was offered a position in the bank. He was paid a handsome salary so that he could adequately support my mother and myself, for I soon put in an appearance.'

Sasha let her mind dwell for a moment on poor Sophie Couriol who had had to choose between her lover or her family. No such ultimatum had obviously been forced on Louise. But then, times changed as the years progressed. Had the Couriol family done Louise any favours when they did not oppose her marriage to Phillipe LeBlanc? Emil was speaking again, still with her hand held tightly in his.

'I was thirteen or fourteen when it was discovered that there were considerable amounts of money missing from the bank. By the time it became evident that my father was the culprit, it was too late, even for my mother's sake, or the good name of my family, to cover up for him. My grandfather, who has since died, was the Bank's President and he had called in the Fraud Squad.

'My father was arrested. I suppose it was to his credit that he made a full confession though he wasn't able to make restitution as most of the money was gone. Ugly facts came to light. My father had virtually been living a double life. There were other women, gambling debts, property he had purchased with the bank's money . . .' Emil's voice trailed off.

'Oh, Emil,' Sasha breathed, 'I'm so sorry.'

Emil gave her a sharp look.

'I have not told you everything,' he declared, 'not nearly everything.'

'Go on,' Sasha urged gently.

'My father was tried and found guilty of embezzlement and fraud. He got an eight-year jail sentence.'

Suddenly the pressure of Emil's fingers on hers caused Sasha to wince, but he didn't seem to notice. As the grip was slowly released, Sasha withdrew her hand gently, rubbing at her fingers. Then with equal gentleness she placed her own hand over Emil's and held it there. She could sense the tension in his rigid body and she desperately wanted to take hold of him, to cradle his head against her. But she was not prepared for his next outburst.

'The punishment was not enough. What were eight years out of his life? Six and a half, as it turned out, because he was released early, for good behaviour. Isn't that what they call it?'

Emil turned dark, angry eyes on Sasha and she recoiled slightly. She had never seen him angry before.

'Was it good behaviour to put my mother through years of torment and terror? Was he indulging in good behaviour when he beat and abused her, taunted and humiliated her? Maman had to serve a life sentence as Phillipe LeBlanc's wife. He should have had to do the same, but unfortunately he was never charged with those offences against my mother. No-one knew of her years of suffering. Not even I did until I was into my teens. To my everlasting shame, I did nothing to ease her suffering. Oh, I tried in my own feeble way, but it was never enough.'

'Did your father ever . . .'

Sasha broke off, unable to finish her question, but Emil knew what she had been about to ask. He shook his head.

'No,' he said, 'my father never laid a finger on me, not even when I tried so futilely to stop him hurting Maman. But, don't you see, Sasha, that only made things worse? My father wanted me to love him. He always made a great show of affection for me, buying me expensive gifts I didn't want or need.'

Emil smiled briefly.

'With the bank's money, no doubt. He was always so full of camaraderie for me, but I grew to hate him, and yes, to fear him, for his moods were always dangerously unpredictable.'

He paused and Sasha sat unmoving, waiting for him to continue.

'To bring the story up to date, we heard of my father's release from prison and abruptly the good years for my mother came to an end.

The old fears returned, the nightmares, the dread of leaving the house. Maman used to sit sometimes for hours, in the dark, waiting for that knock on the door or ring of the telephone that would mean her husband was back in her life, because neither of us doubted that he would try to make contact. So that's when my mother asked my aunts if we could live at their house for a while.'

That part of the story Sasha already knew. And now Louise's strange behaviour was fully explained. Emil was speaking again, gently putting his arm around Sasha's shoulders.

'And I met you, ma petite, during that glorious summer.'

And now the rest of the story must be unfolded Sasha believed she knew in part what Emil would tell her.

'One afternoon, soon after I sent you my grandmother's ring, I returned to Aux Camelias after a trip to Vannes, to find my mother in a terrible state. She had improved so much during our stay in Brittany. I truly believed it wouldn't be long before I would be able to leave her and travel to England to be with you. My Great Aunts would be returning from Scandinavia and she could be with them. Of course I wanted Maman to be at our wedding, and I knew that this was what she wanted, too. I knew also that I would have to tell you the truth about my father, but I was waiting for the right time to do that.

'On that day, I found my mother locked in her bedroom afraid to come out. When eventually I persuaded her to do so, I found her shaking and distressed, her face ravaged by tears. I knew even before she told me that my father had somehow found out where we were and paid us a visit. I wanted to kill him.

'I'm afraid that unintentionally I added to my mother's terror by shaking her and demanding to know where my father was, but she didn't know. All she could tell me was that he had promised to return. He wanted to see me, he said. She couldn't keep him from his son. He blamed my mother for his incarceration. In fact he blamed her for everything that had gone wrong in his life.'

Emil paused and Sasha asked quietly, 'Did your father hurt your mother physically yet again that day?'

Emil gave her a strange look.

'No, he didn't, but what difference does that make? Maman feared for her life, and I don't mind admitting that I, too, was very scared. So we had no choice but to move again. My mother was extremely ill, but we left that same day. I didn't have time to write to you or make a phone call or anything. For reasons I'm not quite sure of, I decided to bring my mother to Switzerland. And it wasn't long before I had to reluctantly have her admitted to a clinic. All my life, my thoughts, my entire being were centred on Maman, Sasha, and all the time there was this constant fear that my father would find us again. I began to feel it was Maman and me against the world. Can you understand that?'

'Yes, of course.'

Impulsively Sasha reached up and kissed Emil's cheek.

'But how is your mother now, Emil?'

'She's much improved, though she won't leave the clinic. She says she doesn't yet have the confidence to do so. Phillipe LeBlanc is out there somewhere. She can never forget that. Nor can I, and I believe he is now a dangerous obsessive. My mother was never more than a voluntary patient and as the clinic is more like a luxury hotel, just outside the city, in acres of private grounds, Maman feels very secure there. She will want to see you, Sasha, I know she will.'

A note of excitement had entered his voice. Sasha wanted to see Louise as well, but at the moment she needed to know clearly in her mind just how she and Emil stood. For her part, she was absolutely determined that she would never let him out of her sight again, but how did he feel? He had just admitted that his mother was his main, his only concern.

It was now twelve months since Emil and Louise had fled to Switzerland. Could their fear of Phillipe LeBlanc still be justified? Wasn't it more likely that he had long since given up all hope of finding out their whereabouts? And there was one even more pressing question which now seemed to force itself from her lips.

'Did you ever think of me at all, Emil, during the last year?'

The look he gave her was one of disbelief that she could ask such a question.

'Sasha, of course, I did! You were constantly in my mind. Did I give you the impression you weren't? You'll never know how many times I sat with a pen in my hand and blank paper before me. Or how many times I started to write "My Darling Sasha," or "My Dearest Love", only to throw the paper away. You see, I didn't know what to say, and the longer I left it, the worse it became. I kept telling myself, "It won't be long now. Maman will get well and my father will no longer be a threat. I can go to Sasha. I can explain everything. She will understand".'

'Of course I would have,' Sasha cried. 'I do.'

'I love you so much!' Emil said hoarsely.

'And I love you.'

'And I'm so sorry I left it up to you to find me like this. But I give you my word, we won't be parted again, ever. I'm only grateful you showed more guts and tenacity than I did. You never gave up, did you, my darling?'

Sasha smiled, too.

'Never!' she said fervently.

They looked at once another for a long moment. Sasha's heart was swelling with happiness. She knew then that everything would come right, not only for her and Emil, but for Louise, too.

When Emil drew her close and put his lips to hers, she responded with all the pent up emotion her body contained. The sweetness of Emil's kisses gave her a heady feeling, as though she was drowning in a sea of love. If she was, then she welcomed such a state. She embraced it fully. The pressure of Emil's mouth became hard.

Then she gave a little start as something leaped up on to the couch by her side, something black and soft, rubbing itself against her legs. She stared. A beautiful young black cat had appeared from nowhere, coming, Sasha now saw, from the half open door. She laughed.

'Oh, my goodness! This isn't BonBon, is it?'

'One and the same,' Emil said.

He released Sasha and gathered the cat into his arms.

'Isn't she beautiful? We brought her with us. We were both far too attached to her to leave her behind.'

Sasha stroked the glossy black fur and heard BonBon's pleasurable purring.

'Lucky black cat,' she murmured.

Emil gave her a solemn look.

'Let's hope so!' he said.

CHAPTER ELEVEN

As Emil had said, the Belvedere Clinic was more like a luxury hotel, set as it was in acres of parkland on the outskirts of Lucerne. At this time of year the snow dazzled across the grounds in unbroken swathes. And to add to the drama and beauty was the backdrop of snow-covered mountains. The air, as Sasha and Emil stepped out of his small black car, was crystal-pure and bitingly cold.

'It's all so beautiful!' Sasha breathed.

'In summer, too,' Emil said, 'when everywhere is green, but there is still snow to be seen on the highest peaks.'

Sasha looked at him, beginning to feel nervous now she was so close to meeting Louise again. Each time she looked at him she seemed to fall even deeper in love with him, if that were possible. They had been together less than twenty-four hours, but already the memory of the months of loneliness, fear and frustration seemed to be fading. It was as though they had never been parted.

'Would you like to live in Switzerland on a permanent basis?' she asked.

Emil immediately sensed what her feelings were. He smiled and gently patted her cold pink cheek.

'Much as I love it here,' he began, 'France is

my home, mine and Maman's and, of course, I hope it will also be yours, Sasha. There is the bank in Paris. I have a responsible position there.'

'So that's what you do for a living,' Sasha teased. 'Didn't you imply that you were a playboy?'

Emil arched his eyebrows.

'I hope I didn't!' he declared. Then seriously he went on, 'we shall return to Paris, ma petite, soon, I hope and pray. Then our life together will really begin.'

Sasha asked something then that had been on her mind ever since she and Emil were re-united.

'If I hadn't found you, Emil, do you think you would eventually have come after me?'

As soon as the words were out, Sasha wished them unsaid. Emil caught hold of her shoulders in the now familiar way he had, so that she was forced to look up into his face. She saw his love for her, the expression in his dark eyes that told her so much and she felt mean because she had asked such a question. Hadn't she told him over and over again that she understood why he had acted as he had? Didn't they both want so very badly to forget the past and look only to the future?

'Sasha,' Emil began, 'I will tell you this now and you must believe me, because if you don't, how can you become my wife? You will never know, my darling, how sorry I am that I hurt you so much or how much I regret how circumstances seemed to take over my life and carry me along, like a twig in a mountain stream. I was helpless. But I would never have let you go out of my life for ever. As soon as Maman was completely well, as soon as the problem of Phillipe LeBlanc was finally over, I would have come to you and, no matter if you'd moved to the ends of the earth, I would have found you, just as you found me.'

'But you're glad I came to you, aren't you?' Still Sasha pressed on, as they stood there in the cold sunshine. She had to have her say and then mention it no more. For answer, Emil kissed her mouth, giving gentle warmth to her chilly lips.

'Yes, I am glad, and I shall thank God every day that you found me.'

It was enough. She put her arms around him and held her face close against his.

'I love you, Emil,' was all she said.

'And now,' Emil's voice had lightened, 'let's go in to Maman, shall we?'

Sasha realised with a jolt that she still had one more barrier to get over.

* * *

Louise had her own suite of rooms in the clinic—sitting-room, bedroom and bathroom, very luxuriously appointed, seeming to deny completely that this was a clinic for people with emotional and psychological problems. In fact the whole of the clinic, or as much as Sasha saw of it, resembled a fine hotel, inside as well as outside.

Louise herself, to Sasha's eyes, appeared remarkably well. She was wearing a dark green dress with a small neat white collar and a row of small buttons down to the waist. Her tawny hair, as Sasha remembered it, was fastened back with a slide, and she had put on make-up, which enhanced her lovely eyes and brought a becoming blush of colour to her cheeks. She was expecting them, as Emil had telephoned her earlier, and she welcomed Sasha with open arms.

'Sasha, my dear,' she cried, 'how nice to see you. Are you well?'

She held Sasha an arm's length away, studying her thoughtfully.

'Very well,' Sasha nodded, 'and you?'

Louise's smile was serene.

'I am very well also.'

She urged Sasha and Emil to take off their coats and sit down, which they did.

'I was so thrilled when Emil told me you were in Lucerne. I can't tell you how sorry I am that you have been so worried and hurt by what happened. But I'm sure Emil has explained and we are forgiven, n'est ce pas?'

'Of course,' Sasha said.

'Now all I look forward to is going home and seeing you and Emil married.'

There was no sign of emotional distress in Louise's voice, and looking into her eyes, Sasha saw how candid and direct her gaze was. No looking away; no strangeness.

'You're sure you want to go back to Paris?' Sasha said.

'Yes, I'm sure.'

Louise turned to the silent Emil and held out her hand to him, which he took hold of gently.

'I can talk freely of my troubles, Sasha. I want no secrets from you, not any more. I owe it to you, to your future together as man and wife, to lay my ghosts once and for all. I have been thinking very carefully during these past few days.'

She looked from one to the other of them, still holding her son's hand.

'I want to go home, but more than that I want to make contact with your father, Emil. I want to . . .'

Emil's eyes widened with alarm as he broke in, 'But, Maman, you mustn't.'

Louise held up her free hand.

'Yes, Emil, mon cheri, I must. It is the only way. I have gone over and over in my mind what happened that day Phillipe came to see me at Aux Camelias. There are some things I never told you. I over-reacted. The very sight of him, the suppressed fears I had held back for so long made my whole being dissolve with terror, but now, now I know there was no need. Phillipe made no threat against me that day.'

Emil looked as though he didn't believe a word his mother was saying.

'But you were out of your mind with fear, Maman,' he reminded her.

Louise smiled.

'You're right, I was, and you, my wonderful son, rushed to protect me, but really all Phillipe wanted was to see you. Oh, he did get angry, but only when I cowered away from threats that were present only in my own mind. He was different. I can admit that now. He's getting married again, to a woman he met through the prison visitors' service. He's got a job, as editor on a small magazine. They know all about his past and he's been given a second chance. So, you see, Emil, I ... we ... must also give him a second chance.'

Sasha was stunned and could think of nothing to say, but Emil pulled free of Louise's hand and began to pace around the room and Sasha could see he was angry and agitated.

'Are you forgetting, Maman, that you begged me to take you away from Aux Camelias? That we left that same night? That I brought you here and that I deserted Sasha because of you!'

He swung round to face his mother.

'Why haven't you told me all this about my father before?'

'In the beginning, you are right, I was ill,

terrified. All I could think of was how your father had treated me in the past. Of how he had ruined my life, and yours. It has taken the months I have been here to build up my confidence, to finally deal with my terror and to remember rationally and clearly how my last meeting with Phillipe really was. I've wanted to tell you a few times, but I couldn't bring myself to do so.'

She looked at Sasha.

'It has taken Sasha's courage and determination to make me see my own situation clearly. We must all make a fresh start, Emil, and to do so I have to finally come to terms with what happened between your father and me. I want to see him. I know where he is.'

'You do?' Emil said in astonishment. 'You told me you didn't.'

'He gave me his business card. It's at Aux Camelias. I hid it at the back of a drawer. I never even looked at it, but now I want to.'

'And you hope I will embrace my father and tell him all is forgiven, I suppose?'

'Not straight away, no. I know that isn't possible. I have no wish to excuse or condone how your father treated me in the past, or how he betrayed my family's trust in him. Phillipe doesn't ask us to forget. He is aware of his past sins as we are, but he needs to know we can at least wish him luck for his future.'

CHAPTER TWELVE

Emil's mouth was tight. 'Well, I don't know if I can do that, Maman,' he said. 'All this is a terrible shock to me. I have seen you almost destroy yourself because of that man. I can't for the life of me think how you can now make such a complete turn about.'

'Because I want peace, Emil. I want to live in the city I love without fear. I want to see you and Sasha married. I want to hold my grandchild in my arms.'

'It will be my father's grandchild, too,' Emil reminded her. 'Have you given that any thought?'

'Phillipe is moving to America. His wife-to-be is American by birth though she has lived most of her life in France. After we've made our peace with him, we don't ever have to see him again.'

'And what if he's already gone to America?' Emil asked.

'That is a possibility, of course, but at least, I will have tried,' Louise said determinedly.

There was a silence. Emil looked at his hands. His brow was furrowed. Sasha could see he was battling with his turmoil of inner feelings, trying to reach some sort of decision.

It wasn't easy for him, but suddenly, clearly, Sasha knew that Louise's way was the only way. She had to go through with it. And they had to be with her, to encourage and support her.

And then, they could get on with the rest of their lives.

She moved nearer to Emil on the couch, putting her arm around his bent shoulders.

'Emil, darling, you know your mother is right. She wants no more of looking over her shoulder, of hiding, of running. And, goodness knows, I want to put down roots myself. For the past eighteen months I don't know whether I've been on my head or my heels.'

She spoke the last words light-heartedly because suddenly that was how she felt.

They could all face the future with confidence now. Emil turned to her and he, too, was smiling.

'All right, my dearest Sasha, you win,' he conceded. 'I can see with two women in my life I had better learn to do as I am told.'

Louise rose from her chair and rushed to embrace her son, kissing him on both cheeks. Sasha patted his shoulder, reassuringly.

'Only two women?' she teased. 'Aren't you reckoning without my mother?'

Emil groaned and Louise laughed. Sasha realised it was probably the first time she had heard her laugh. It was a wonderful sound.

We hope you have enjoyed this Large Print book. Other Chivers Press or G.K. Hall & Co. Large Print books are available at your library or directly from the publishers.

For more information about current and forthcoming titles, please call or write, without obligation, to:

Chivers Press Limited
Windsor Bridge Road
Bath BA2 3AX
England
Tel. (01225) 335336

OR

G.K. Hall & Co.
P.O. Box 159
Thorndike, Maine 04986
USA
Tel. (800) 223-2336

All our Large Print titles are designed for easy reading, and all our books are made to last.

FEB 29 2000 BY

PQ
19.95
2.00
LP
MCFADDEN
Erene

DATE DUE	
APR 0 3 2000	
APR 2 4 2000	
MAY 0 3 2000	
MAY 1 5 2002	
AUG 1 5 2002	
MAR 2 0 2003	
OCT 1 0 2003	
MAY 0 4 2005 DM	
APR 2 3 2009 W	
MAR 2 4 2010	
APR 0 5 2010	
FEB 0 8 2011	
FEB 2 3 2011 MB	
GAYLORD	PRINTED IN U.S.A.